PRAISE FOR

Mrs. Bennet Has Her Say

"*Mrs. Bennet Has Her Say* is, like its author, uproarious and savvy and wild. If Jane Austen had been allowed to write about sex, I'd like to think this is how she would have done it: with irreverence and wit, showing us how sexual politics might set not just a marriage, but an entire family, on an irreversible course. A delight on every level."

—Rebecca Makkai, author of *The Borrower* and *The Hundred-Year House*

"As we have come to expect, Jane Juska's wit and insight once again show us our foibles and humanity while entertaining us on every page."

—Kelly Corrigan, *New York Times* bestselling author of *The Middle Place* and *Glitter and Glue*

"*Mrs. Bennet Has Her Say* is the witty and ribald mother-from-hell prequel that fans of Jane Austen have been waiting for."

—Mark Haskell Smith author of *Raw: A Love Story*

"Funny and irreverent (a trademark of Jane Juska). *Mrs. Bennet Has Her Say* is an intimate look into the marriage of literature's most mismatched couple. I loved it! A lot! If it goes to series, I want in. I'll learn the accent."

—Sharon Gless

PRAISE FOR

A Round-Heeled Woman

"Feisty, charming, moving, and wise, this page-turner of a memoir proves that life for a woman—sexual and otherwise—hardly stops at thirty-nine."

—Cathi Hanauer, editor of *The Bitch in the House*

"Juska writes well about the sex . . . but even better about the seductions, which take on the luster of years served. Expressive and touching: Readers will be rooting for Juska to get all that she wants." —*Kirkus Reviews*

"There's something universal in [Juska's] love affair with the written word." —*Publishers Weekly*

"[A] thoroughly engaging memoir . . . Refreshingly honest, remarkably candid." —*Booklist*

Mrs. Bennet Has Her Say

JANE JUSKA

BERKLEY BOOKS, NEW YORK

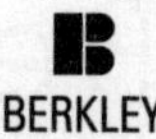

An imprint of Penguin Random House LLC
375 Hudson Street, New York, New York 10014

This book is an original publication of Penguin Random House LLC.

Library of Congress Cataloging-in-Publication Data

Juska, Jane.
Mrs. Bennet has her say / Jane Juska. — Berkley trade paperback edition.
p. cm.
ISBN 978-0-425-27843-7 (softcover)
1. Young women—England—Fiction. 2. England—Social life and customs—18th century—Fiction. I. Austen, Jane, 1775–1817. Pride and prejudice. II. Title.
PS3610.U875M77 2015 2014048297
813'.6—dc23

PUBLISHING HISTORY
Berkley trade paperback edition / August 2015

PRINTED IN THE UNITED STATES OF AMERICA

10 9 8 7 6 5 4 3 2 1

Cover art by Andrew Bannecker.
Cover design by Judith Lagerman.
Interior text design by Laura K. Corless.
Interior hat ornaments © venimo / Shutterstock.com.

Penguin
Random
House

To William

Mrs. Bennet Has Her Say

Ch. 1

In May by Candlelight at Brighton, 1785

Dear Jane,

O la! If only poor Mother had lived to tell me of the infamy that would be my wedding night. I recall, dear sister, when soon after your own marriage you tried to warn me of what lay in store: We were upstairs in my own dear little room which looked over the town square. Suddenly you pulled me to the window and said, "Look there." I did as you asked but saw nothing unusual, only a few dogs playing about. "Look at those two," you said. "What?" I wondered and then—I shudder to recall—my glance fell upon a pair of dogs, one on his hind legs clasping the rear quarters of the other, all a-quiver. Suddenly he ceased his jittering and returned to ground. It was clear from the rigid portion of this agitator that he was a male, the victim female. I hoped never to see such a sight again. Alas, 'twas not to be.

Something of this I knew to be my fate; I have, after all, reached the proper age of fifteen. And so I kept in my mind that the female dog did not die, though she seemed to take no pleasure from the encounter or to have a choice as to whether or not to participate. Still, she continued on her way afterward with no signs of the ravage that had befallen her. Small comfort.

Brighton is a lovely place. Our (that odious pronoun) inn borders the sea and I can see ships far off on the horizon, and on the promenade couples and families on holiday. One couldn't wish for a prettier place in which to begin one's life as a married woman, which, forever and a day, is what I am. I could enjoy myself if it weren't for the man who is my husband and who appears to be a satyr. He seems to believe that I am his to muss and turn this way and that and up-end at will. He seems to believe it his right to do this at any time of the day or night and often both and sometimes twice in one lying! Surely, dear sister, this frequency is unusual; had you suffered as I do surely you would have warned me.

Here—for writing is my only friend at present—is my wedding night. Wedded bliss it was not. He had been watching me from the darkness and now, his breath heavy from wine, he ordered me to unloose my stays (a not altogether unwelcome command, for as you and I know, stays can bind and even cut when worn overlong). I did as I was told and stood silent in my petticoat, feet bare, arms crossed over my bosom. He dropped his trousers and oh, dear sister, you as a married woman would not be surprised I do not think. But, despite the blissful memories of my beloved colonel, memories I have shared with you, such a sight was new to me; indeed, I had scarcely seen or felt the colonel's entry, so impassioned had I become from the sensation that his voice and his lips and his touch inspired in me. Clearly, marriage does not require such tenderness, although I was ignorant of that as well. And so the little shriek I uttered from surprise and apprehensiveness Mr. Bennet took as my expression of delight because he grinned and advanced, calling out, "Consummate!" Why he should summon the broth that Mother provided us when we were sickly I have no idea, and so I leapt onto the bed and attempted to cover myself with the bedclothes. But he grabbed them, threw them from me, and straddled me, his manhood seeking its inevitable way up and under my underthings, muttering "Consummate" as he did. All night long and into the morning he was at me—it certainly did not take that dog so long—until he fell off me and to sleep. I followed him shortly for I, too, was exhausted.

To be fair, I must say that despite my protestations, I could not help but admire his energy and his determination, at least in retrospect. And I was grateful to him: after such a night no woman could forestall motherhood, and Mr. Bennet's paternity would never be questioned, because if anyone had ever been consummated it was I.

I did not bleed, dear sister, and my husband promises to make much of that, so I must dissemble so convincingly that he believes that my pleasure exceeded any pain and injury I might have suffered in my virgin state. I will not tell him—I cannot tell him!—that I did indeed bleed but not on this night. No, not on his night, but on the night of my true marriage (albeit without benefit of clergy) to Colonel Millar those many months ago.

All this you know, but it helps me during this time of despair to recall our meeting, how I stood with all the pretty maidens along the road as the militia in all their splendour marched into Meryton. And how, soon after, their leader, beautiful in his military regalia, black hair, flashing eyes, and oh so tall, stood before me. What can he want? I wondered. And he said, "I am a stranger here and lonely. Would you walk with me about the village on this fine day?" Oh yes, I would and I did. We continued to walk until darkness fell. Tired, we fell upon the grass next to the river, where we lay side by side until he leaned over and kissed me, oh so gently, and oh so gently pressed his hand upon my skirts and then beneath them. You know, dear sister, what came next. I was deflowered and blissfully so. I do not recall returning home; I am certain he escorted me there. I do recall the devastation I felt when I learned soon thereafter that his regiment had been called to another town. At least I have the memories and, truth to tell, a bit more.

But ah, how I thought of my dear colonel during this everlasting wedding night and blessed the memory of his kisses and gentle touches that carried me through the misery of my debut as Mrs. Edward Bennet.

Oh dear, I must close, dear Jane, for he is come upon me again.

Your loving sister,
Marianne

Verbis, quae timido quoque possent addere mentem.

"Words which would have inspired
the greatest coward."

—HORACE

I, Edward Bennet, begin this journal in order to record the events of my life such as they occurred in this year of 1785, the year in which I took myself a wife. Such a momentous occasion is deserving of my considered attention, and this journal will bear witness to my efforts in that direction.

And, should I choose to continue those efforts beyond this year, this journal will also serve as a history of myself for those of my descendants who wish to delve into their beginnings. And of course they will, if only the boys, my direct heirs.

First, some explanation of my life as it preceded my marriage. I have always been a retiring sort of fellow, more interested in books than in parties, more at home in the country than in the town. I grew into manhood in this very home, Longbourn, a respectable red-brick with a respectable cook and housekeeper and a manservant for myself, in the midst of green meadows, a pretty forest, trails for walking, a brook for fishing, all the beauty the English countryside offers. I was content.

However, not long after reaching my majority, I faced the necessity of finding a wife even though I was perfectly happy in my library and on my ambles about the property. I looked into my future with apprehension. Should I remain single and childless, my property, entailed as it was, would fall to my closest male heir, in this case a cousin, a Mr. Collins. In truth, I came to detest Mr. Collins, and as he grew in years and in health, I lived each day in the fear that should he so choose, in the absence of male heirs, Longbourn would be his and my family cast out. The very thought that Collins might someday stroll about the grounds of this, my home, was intolerable. Action, never my natural inclination, seemed called for, and so reluctantly I left Longbourn, though never for very long, and ventured into nearby Meryton, where, I had been given to understand, marriageable girls waited in every parlour and at every ball. It appeared that I would have to learn to dance.

Ch. 2

A Tuesday in May at Longbourn

Dear Jane,

Do you remember as fondly as I the dancing in the town hall? It is the very hall where your beloved Mr. Phillips proposed to you beneath the trees which lined the path where the two of you wandered. I recall Mother worrying that Mr. Phillips was only a clerk. How pleased you must be that he has become the attorney that our father was, his office occupying the very space as that of our dear papa. Oh, that Father had lived! He might well have warned me off entering into a loveless marriage. Still, I suppose he would have seen Mr. Bennet as upright and as responsible as any suitor could be, the holder of property, a man entirely suitable for his daughter. But of course, were I to confess—as I always do to you, dear sister—I would admit that fortune smiled on me, perhaps in recompense for the terror that struck when my monthly flux ceased. I will not trouble you with the memory of we two in the shameful corner of my little bedroom where I told you my fears. So while I cannot bring myself to think of Mr. Bennet as a godsend, I must admit that he was a bit of luck and came, as they say, "in the nick of time."

Can you hear my sigh, dear sister?

Until he stumbled against me during the minuet—how anyone could trip over his own feet in such a simple dance is beyond me—I was barely aware of this fellow, who on first glance and first dance was clearly from the country. The word "bumpkin" comes to mind. My attention was absorbed by the presence of Colonel Millar far across the room, who gazed at me with the utmost fondness—surely my due—and whose name was next on my dance card. Taller than Papa, his eyes as black as his moustache, his smile warm and inviting, he bowed slightly in my direction, and my heart beat faster. The dance would be a gavotte, my favourite, particularly so with the colonel, who would be the lead man, of course, and who at the end, as tradition would have it, must kiss his partner. Oh, please let me not stumble or, worse, perspire. Happily, I had brought with me a second pair of gloves, which would replace those which this Mr. Bennet had soiled with the moisture of exertion from his own hands. Mr. Bennet, if I may be so crude, sweats. Colonel Millar, an officer need I remind you, perspires and that only lightly. I prayed to the heavens above that I would do neither.

I like to think that the colonel took notice of my small waist but could not help but note that his eyes fell most often on my neckline, which, allowed by such social occasions, had dipped somewhat, encouraging a wee bit of peeping from those who would be so bold. Do you recall how tightly we laced our stays so that such peeping would be rewarded? Mother urged us to take up the newer style, which she said was not so heavily boned; she even offered to purchase the new corsets for us. She said they would not so distort us as she assured us they did by narrowing our back and widening our front. But we would not risk the newer and more comfortable strapless stays because they did not make the waist small or push the bosom into amplitude but forced us only to stand with our shoulders back. Fashionable, our mother said. More of her advice we did not heed. Such are daughters, I suppose.

As the gavotte ended and I looked up at the colonel, he leaned down and his lips did not graze my cheek or scuff my ear or touch my brow. His lips met my lips quickly, soft and lightly as a butterfly. Just as quickly he straightened and smiled, holding me by my elbow to steady me as he led me back to you and Mother, and as he assisted me to sit—for it was clear that my head was spinning—he whispered in my ear, “You are a love.” Had it not been for Mother’s suspicious frown, I would have followed him then and there. Alas, my dance card announced the next dance and my next partner: Mr. Bennet again. Mr. Bennet took no notice of my waist; his ogling went directly to my bosom, where it remained throughout the minuet. Subtlety, it would seem, is not his forte.

Even now, some weeks into our marriage, I cannot believe that my life is forever tied to him. I take some comfort in the loveliness of the countryside.

Yrs affectionately,
Marianne

Edward Bennet on His Courting

Quem circumcursans huc atque huc saepe Cupido
Fulgebat crocina splendidus in tunica.

"When Cupid fluttering round me here and there
Shone in his rich purple mantle."

—CATULLUS

Despite my initial awkwardness on the dance floor, I will confess that I was quite admired by the young ladies present. And so I continued with plans to become the father of sons, the caretakers of my old age and of the property that would naturally fall to them. I found the future Mrs. Bennet, née Gardiner, to my liking, in ways similar to the broodmare of which I was at that time particularly fond. Like the pretty little horse, Miss Gardiner had a sprightly manner and hips that promised the birthing of sleek colts; I imagined this exuberant young girl frolicking in the fields behind the barn, she and the mare, together. I imagined myself gazing fondly at the scene from my library, then turning to my books, which even at my relatively young age numbered, along with those volumes attained by my father, in the hundreds. Ah yes, I could imagine that her 4,000 pounds per annum might serve even to add to my collection. My own 2,000 was barely sufficient to keep a few servants, but Miss Gardiner, I could see, was young and strong and would not require a large household staff. I decided to ask for her hand in marriage.

June, from Longbourn

My dear Jane,

What a fine sister you are! Too late I have come across the little book you handed me when I was but fourteen. As I did all good sense, I set it aside when you offered it to me and now, of course, it is too late. Allow me to point out those Hints, as they are titled in this little book, so that should you have daughters, they will be made aware of pitfalls and so avoid the errors of my recent past. I know that you yourself must have made use of it, as your Mr. Phillips is a living example of the ideal man revealed in those chapters, which guide us, as they say, on our Journey to the Land of Hymen. I need not tell you that guidance of this sort ought be made available to all young women as they are made aware of their future role as wives and mothers. I have copied out some of it for you:

1) If the man have thick, red lips, he will be simple, good-natured, and easily managed.

2) If he speak quick but distinct, and walk firm and erect, he will be ambitious, active, and probably a good husband.

That, my dear sister, describes my colonel, not my husband. The following is more characteristic of Mr. Bennet:

3) If he speak and look with his mouth extended, it is a certain mark of stupidity.
4) If he be beetle-browed, it shows duplicity and fickleness.

Now, I know you are saying that Mr. Bennet is not as repulsive as all that and reluctantly I would have to agree: He is not stupid even though his lips are thin and lacking in colour, with occasional spittle in the corners. He as yet reveals no fickleness; indeed, he is more faithful more frequently than I would have it. I do not yet know about his duplicity, although his calls for repeated lovemaking, as he would call it, would suggest a certain dishonesty. But then, I suppose one could call me duplicitous as well, for I married as a virgin, withholding from him the secret only you and I share. Still, had I been apprised of such honest words as these Hints offer, I might not have agreed so readily to marry the man who is the source of my constant sorrow.

My dear sister, I am with child. But then we knew that, didn't we.

Yr sister,
Marianne

Dear Jane,

Thank you for your good wishes and your sound advice. I hope Mr. Phillips has got over his cold. Mr. Bennet remains in perfect health. My sniffles have come from within for I have spent many secret hours in tears, though none of them in Mr. Bennet's presence. He is not a cruel man, but he is without that which would allow him to apprehend my sadness. I hesitate to say something so harsh about the man who is my husband, but he is without feeling, at least when it comes to me. His sympathies are great for his horses, especially the foals, and for the old dog who follows him everywhere. I cannot recall a single time when he has looked directly into my eyes; his own dart about every which way and light only on my belly where my child grows with each passing day. Often I wonder if he is simply shy in my presence, but I cannot know, for there is no conversation between us. And no smiles. In the evening, after supper, he repairs to his library. I sit by the fire sewing tiny clothes for the baby until the fading of the light.

He lights our way upstairs with nary a word or even a nod. Could it be that he regrets his insatiability? That I remind him of his coarser nature? Well, there is no sense in pursuing answers. It is time to dry my tears.

I will send to the village for the name of a midwife to assist me when my time is nigh. I have decided to keep my expectations from Mr. Bennet for the time being; he could very well question the speediness with which I have become pregnant; after all, it has been not even one month since our marriage. Of course, he would put it up to his potency, and yet one can never be sure of this man. When he is not turning from me, his face dark with concentration on one of his books, he is mercurial: laughing, flailing his extremities, galumphing across the bed (and me), his eyes aglow with lust, a terrifying sight. Even during daylight hours I cannot so much as cross from one side of the room to the other without his grabbing at my petticoat and shoving his hands, which for a man who does no manual labour whatsoever are surprisingly coarse and rough, beneath my chemise. And he seems not to care if his behaviour is witnessed by others! Only the other day, whilst I was consulting with Cook in the pantry, in he stormed and all but tossed me onto the counter, where he lifted up my petticoat and began to rummage. The shame of it seems always to be mine, never his. Also the cleaning up after. Cook refuses to come near.

When he is not asserting his dominion in the bedchamber or the parlour or even the kitchen, he sulks, is surly in manner, broods, and spends much time in his library—where, not surprisingly, I am not allowed to go. On the rare occasions that he takes a stroll about his property I do enter the library and have found there many books about the creatures that live nearby, a very fat book called *The Sermons of John Donne*, whose very title puts me off, but also some novels! O la! One such is *Pamela* by a Mr. Samuel Richardson. Although Mother taught us to read when we were but small, she forbade either of us to read that very book; but now that I am a married woman, she could have no objections. Mr. Bennet is fastidious about the arrangement of his books so I have been very careful to tuck the book beneath my skirt so that no servant can notice and then to return it to its proper place before Mr. Bennet returns. O Jane! It affords me such pleasure even for so short a time. Here is her story: Pamela, a young servant girl, is pursued by an older and titled man. Oh, Jane, she is only fifteen years of age—as am I—and she vows to lose her life before her virtue. I will her to succeed; however, I have read only to page 9 of the first folio and cannot imagine her maintaining her purity for another 400 pages! We shall have to see; in the meantime, she brings me great delight. I am her champion on every page. She is my friend.

I must hush, here he comes.

Yrs affectly,
Marianne

Reflections on Married Life

Natura homo nundum et elgans animal est.

"Man is by nature a clean and delicate creature."

—SENECA

I was for a time a happy man. I found my wife much to my liking. Her nether regions were plump and promised the sons who would, I was certain, resemble myself in appearance and temperament; that is, they would have my broad forehead and strong jaw; they would have my love for the animals of the field and the birds of the air. They would grow into manhood appreciative of their rights as gentlemen and landholders of this most agreeable property which I have spent much time contemplating from the windows of my library. It would not be long now, given my unceasing efforts, until fruitfulness would show itself in the person of a son. I would perhaps have to cease and desist in the delights of matrimonial concupiscence, at least until nature had done its duty, but, and here I sighed, 'twas a small price to pay for so rewarding a return. After that, back to business. I smoothed my trouser flap at the thought.

A Summer Evening at Longbourn

Dear Jane,

It is hands off for Mr. Bennet now that I have informed him of my condition. He was at once so happy and so proud I could not but help myself in smiling at this man who has done so much to make himself loathsome to me. He is like a boy in his delight and at the same time, for the first moment since our marriage, solicitous of me and my comfort. Nothing will do but that I sit instead of stand, that I leave off any thought of the kitchen or of the housekeeping; and under no circumstances am I to ride in the carriage. He has even hired an upstairs maid and a housekeeper who will take over the management of this house. I will admit coming to this marriage ill-equipped to direct the two servants who reside here, but now, with the addition of Mrs. Rummidge, who appears good-natured and capable, I can attend more closely to my burgeoning self.

I find, dear Jane, that I am enjoying this pregnancy. It is a relief not to be pursued but attended to. It is pleasurable to have time to wander about this glorious countryside. Against Mr. Bennet's advice—he fears I will stumble and fall so is happiest when I am still—I stroll along what I have come to call the Wood Walk bordered by copsewood and timber, beneath its shelter primroses, anemones, and wild hyacinths. It is so lovely and untouched. The other day I found a bird's nest upon the ground and quickly returned it to a low-lying branch of an alder. When I mentioned having done so to Mr. Bennet he scolded me that I had contaminated the nest. Then he warned that I must never be so careless of my own nest, and he made me sit down in the parlour all alone for what seemed like an hour "to contemplate the seriousness of your behaviour, my dear." Pfah, it is my nest, not his. I will wander where I like until such time as my condition prevents my doing so. I am after all about to turn sixteen.

Do you have news of Colonel Millar's regiment?

The Frustrations of Married Life

Humani a se nihil alienum putet.

"Let him not think himself exempt from that which is incidental to other men."

—TERENCE

Bored with the interminable wait for the birth of my son, I contemplated taking on a few students. One or two might provide me with companionship and serve to enliven my mind, dulled by the banality of my wife's pregnancy and by her constant good cheer. To my dismay, she has refused my advice on comportment during her gestation and will walk about the countryside at will, eat puddings doused with treacle, ingest great quantities of beef roast, and even wild blackberries picked during her peregrinations. She lumbers about the house clutching a wedge of Cheddar, and on one occasion I discovered her sipping from a glass of brandy taken from my very own cellar where I have forbidden her to go! She grows ever larger in the belly. The encroachment of her cheeks over the entirety of her face obscures what had been a twinkle in the eye and remains barely a glint. She speaks rarely to me although I detected a small smile over some amusement kept entirely to herself. She appears to be living a life far removed from me and over which I have no say whatsoever. I find myself living with a stranger and I must confess to being lonely.

Before the New Year, at Longbourn

Dear Jane,

Oh, how I wish I could have been with you and Mr. Phillips for this Christmas season, my first as a married woman and heavy with child to boot. But, as you know from Mr. Bennet's greeting to you in early December, it is best that I not travel—or do much of anything else if you would know the truth. I am inclined to wish that he were still bedeviling me to conceive; at least, when 'twas done, 'twas done. Now he hovers; he never leaves my side, not in the day, not at night. He is forever pulling up footstools, has had the carpenter raise my favourite one so that my feet, when Mr. Bennet places them onto it, are level with my hips. "No sense in forcing the little tyke out before his time," he says with a gurgle he believes is a chortle. Believe me, Mr. Bennet is not capable of chortling; gurgling is as close as he can come. And now he does it all the time, believing it to recommend his suitability for fatherhood. I have warned him that the child may not wait the requisite nine months; indeed, that the little tyke, as he would call him, could appear as early as this month. He agrees instantly, eyeing the enormity of my belly. "The sooner the better," he gurgles and rings for Cook to bring me the camomile tea replete with herbs known only to him that he believes will facilitate the birth of his first son. I sip. I know otherwise, of course, and have decided to name her Jane. What better beginning could I bestow upon her than the blessing of the name of one so dear to me. You can be sure I have not consulted Mr. Bennet on this matter. Occasionally I admit to a pang of sympathy; he knows so little of the woman who is his wife. But then he does something like cock-a-doodling about the dining room proclaiming his approaching fatherhood in tones so stentorian that Mrs. Rummidge claps her hands over her ears. You are fortunate that we did not visit you this holiday; there is no telling when Mr. B.'s outbursts will occur or what form they will take. One would think it was he who was carrying a child.

Yrs affectionately,
Marianne

Late December at Longbourn

Dear Jane,

My time is near. The winds howl, snow drifts against the windows; the fierceness of winter threatens our every comfort. How I wish you were here with me. That your duties to your husband overwhelm your love for your sister I well understand. The demands upon our role as wife are not to be denied. I do hope Mr. Phillips regains his health soon. In your absence, Mrs. Rummidge, herself a mother several times over, has summoned a midwife to assist in the birth and lying-in soon to be mine. Mr. Bennet, as you might imagine, is loudly insistent on calling for a doctor when the time is nigh. He has read a monograph on forceps, an ugly-sounding instrument used to draw the baby from the mother should contractions be reduced. A doctor, he insists, would have knowledge of this procedure along with the proper use of opium or chloroform should the pain be too great. I laugh at him. He can read all he likes, know all there is to know, but in this regard I reign supreme. I will not have a doctor or drugs; I will not be bled as he urges, for my humours have never been more balanced than now and my sense of well-being protects me and my baby from the interference of strangers, albeit men of medicine. The very thought of a man present in the birthing chamber repulses me. Mrs. Rummidge, it would seem, agrees with me so wholeheartedly that she would absent herself, too, from my chamber. She who when I first arrived at Longbourn seemed so capable, so comforting, so experienced in the ways of motherhood, has fallen into bits and pieces now that my time is close upon me. She has agreed to boil water though she continues to ask the reason—why ought I to know?—but will leave the rest to me and the midwife. No matter. I am content and confident that my beloved is with me though still so far away.

I have felt the little one moving about for some months now. Much pain awaits me, but I know that the little girl who comes from the deepest part of me will make any discomfort, however severe, momentary. I await her with all the love I can bring to bear. Would it amuse you, as it does me, to know that the name of the midwife, an old woman, her face scoured with wrinkles, and stooped, is Pamela. She seems kind.

Little Jane is on her way. You are about to become an aunt.

"Drat!" This the single utterance from the new father with no acknowledgement of my pain and discomfort in the delivery of his first child. It would seem that I have disappointed him anew.

Ch. 3

The New Year at Longbourn, 1786

Dear Sister,

The winds continue to howl but within all is safe and warm for I have my own darling child nestled close to me. She came easily, so the midwife assured me, and in truth even so close to the birthing I can barely remember the pain. She is beautiful, though of course all mothers say that. And she is good; no one need tell me that. Her little mouth is a rosebud and her tiny fingers grip mine with a strength surprising in one so small. She cries only rarely and then out of hunger. My milk flows boundlessly. Mrs. Rummidge continues to boil water despite my assurances that hot water is no longer necessary and even though Mr. B. has chastised her for steaming up the windows of the entire kitchen, pantry, and hall. I hear him bellowing, "I can write my name on any window in the house! I must wipe them down to see into the fields! Cook has threatened to quit so damp are her bowls and pins and all the things she tells me she needs to keep us well. The laundress no longer starches my shirts. 'No reason to do it,' she says, 'they just go limp.'" Only the sties and coops out back escape the gusts; that is where Mr. B. spends more and more of his time. A good place for him, to my mind.

Most recently, Mrs. Rummidge has confessed to being widowed early on and left childless. "I never did know the least thing about spilling a child. Forgive me, ma'am." She bowed her head, where only a few strands of hair remain, and scrunched up her eyes until the tears came. "But I did want to help, you know," she said wanly. She has given me good reason to let her go. But she is poor, and besides, she plumps my pillows and brings me endless cups of tea and is almost as taken with little Jane as I. "Oh, ma'am, she's a perfect one, she is." And then she brushes my hair off my forehead and with a hand as soft as down smooths my brow. In the absence of dear Mother and of yourself, Mrs. Rummidge will have to do. I am grateful for her ministrations.

Occasionally Mr. Bennet tramps in from the animal pens and peeks into the bedroom, looking perplexed and out of sorts, his usual mien, I might add. He comes no nearer to his daughter than the doorjamb. "All is well?" he mumbles and stomps off to his library without awaiting an answer. And yes, all is well, even with Mr. B. so testy and grim. Inside this room my daughter and I give life to one another.

I will draw out my lying-in period as long as I can, complaining of pain and discomfort in that part of myself where Mr. B. claimed dominion on our wedding night, for I suspect that once he discovers that in truth all is well, he will renew his efforts, perhaps even more frequently, to create the son to which he believes himself entitled. Meanwhile, I am content. This luxury of motherhood will not last, but for the moment, all is well.

Yrs very affec.,
Marianne

On Becoming a Father

Omnia autem quae secundum naturam fiunt,
sunt habenda in bonis.

"All things that are done according to nature
are to be accounted good."

—CICERO

Were it suitable for one of my position to confess to anything, I would confess that this child, this little Jane, my daughter, is quite an extraordinary infant, as of course any child sired by myself would be. Mrs. B. called to me as I stood there in the doorway that already her eyes were turning from blue to some mysterious colour I liked to think was mine, a greenish grey, or would they be brown?—'twas too soon to be certain. Out of respect for my wife's delicate condition, I chose not to enter the room, but try as I might, I could find nowhere in the house safe from the constant crooning of my wife, which for reasons unknown to me caused dyspepsia to rise from within. I quelled my discomfort by reminding myself that only one more month of the drear which sat upon my fields and in my marital bed remained. Then buds of spring would deliver the bounties of nature I so richly deserved. I had not whistled since leaving my boyhood some ten years earlier, but whistling seemed called for now, and so I began.

Then from the bedroom: "The sound you hear, Mr. Bennet, is the clapping of my hands over little Jane's ears." Mrs. Rummidge, having positioned herself at the top of the stairs where I was sure to see her, raised her eyes to heaven and made the sign of the cross. She believes herself to be Irish and the mother of many, hence her claim that she is duty-bound to protect them. A likely story.

May at Longbourn

Dear Jane,

I do believe Mr. Bennet will have his boy. Already the quickening is upon me and the black bile rises daily. He is tumbling within my womb so that I cannot hold down food of the least sort and each morning what little breakfast Mrs. Rummidge has managed to urge upon me spills forth into the basin. Who could have imagined that I would be with child so soon and so miserable. I sense a battle brewing between me and this little one. I am fatigued ever so much sooner in the day than I was with oh so easy little Jane. If this one wears me out before he is even born, what will he do once he is here?

Lest you think me an unworthy mother, please know that I have a mother's love for him despite the discomfort he is thrusting upon me. Yet it is a love different from what I felt for Jane. This little boy comes from my womb but not my soul. His eyes will not be the deep blue of Jane's; he will not have the sweetly firm chin of his sister, nor, clearly, her disposition. This child comes from Mr. Bennet, my lawfully wedded husband, and will have some of Mr. Bennet's traits to be sure. I can only hope they will not include Mr. Bennet's failure to clip from within his nose and ears the unsightly tufts he seems oblivious to. If I did not pull away from him every now and then and scorn his ardent pleadings, insisting that unless he saw to his personal hygiene there would be no continuance of this so-called lovemaking, I am certain that from his face and neck would sprout a veritable vegetable patch much in need of weeding. I may be a dutiful wife but I am not a gardener. "Tend to your garden, Mr. Bennet," I said to him more than once, "if you wish me to be fruitful and multiply." He sighed but obeyed. "With obedience comes reward," I reminded him. And now he claims that my morning sickness serves as proof that he was right. "*Who* was right?" I enquire of him. "Wasn't it I who was right? Was it not I who insisted on clipping and pruning?" He answers as he always does with a twist and a twirl against common sense: "Ah, but my dear, it was I who was obedient." He chuckled. "And it is my child who rests within." Another chuckle. "The child within," I answer, "is not resting, you may be sure of that." "Ah yes"—and he came close to a chortle—"the boy is master even now." Lest you have forgot, Mr. Bennet has three utterances: the chuckle, the growl, and a moanful shudder to signal the end of his interminable lovemaking, the absence of the latter the single advantage of this difficult pregnancy.

Because yes, dear sister, Mr. Bennet and I, always the dutiful wife, did resume relations. Mrs. Rummidge assured me, bless her ignorant heart, that nursing little Jane would ensure that not even the frequent and energetic proddings of Mr. Bennet would end in pregnancy. "Now, ma'am," she said, "believe me. Suckling the little one will deliver you from another babe until such time as you choose." And so Mr. Bennet, whose pacing and growling outside my door I could no longer bear, came into my bed. Shudder and moan, moan and shudder as he tilled his soil, and here I am now, miserable and forlorn, with little Jane not yet even a year.

Do you recall Miss A——, the kind and temperate woman who lived not far from us in Meryton? She who advised us so long ago, "Anything is to be preferred or endured rather than marrying without affection"? Surely she told a truth, but truth does not necessarily rest on fact, in my case the presence of a child within my womb and I without a husband. I wonder if Miss A——, were she to know the facts of my young life, would scorn me or amend her words of wisdom. At the very least, she would preface her statement with "*Almost* anything." . . . Or perhaps not, for Miss A—— never married. So far as we know, she never even fell in love. Alas, wisdom comes at a price. Mine certainly has.

Next month I turn seventeen. I am soon the mother of two and a stranger in this house and to the man who is my husband. I am a stranger to myself. I was too long a child made too soon a woman. What is to become of me?

Yr Marianne

On the Trials of Being a Husband

Mus in pice.

"A mouse in a pitch barrel."

—MONTAIGNE

It is a truth universally acknowledged that every man in possession of a wife must be in want of a son. I take pen in hand to underscore that very conviction and to offer in writing a defense of my own position in a household suddenly and unexpectedly ruled by women. Perhaps one day this record of events will bring into balance the events of my unfortunate married life. Please understand that with the birth of this second child—another girl—I have been twice disappointed. I feel myself punished for something I did not do and was not guilty of and had only the briefest acquaintance with, that being those few moments during which I planted my seed within this same wife who, against my wishes and no doubt due to all her complaining and whining during the nine months of waiting, had the temerity to spew forth yet another girl! Beyond understanding! The world does not need another girl. One is sufficient to carry out the continuation of life as I believe it should be. This second girl, this Elizabeth so-named for no reason I have been made aware of, is an insult.

I keep to my library save for meals, but even there I am not provided with the peaceful comfort I have come to expect because upstairs, from Mrs. Bennet's room, comes the endless squalling of the infant Elizabeth. Morning, noon, night, nothing seems to soothe her, not even my threats. "Do not touch her!" screams Mrs. Bennet from her bed where Elizabeth twists away from her mother's breast to cast an angry eye on the man—her own father!—who looks as if he means to kill her. Devil child! Her hair has already turned red, her only saving grace, my hair having been once that very colour. There are moments, I will admit, when she is not unpleasing to my eye. But her apoplectic behaviour stems certainly from Mrs. Bennet's family; nothing in the history of my own peace-loving family would account for the baleful glare and the ear-splitting yowls that come from this fulvous-faced creature, arms and legs beating the air above her and upon anyone beside her, such as her mother. Only Mrs. Rummidge, unaccountably, can quiet her. "Here, here," she croons as she rocks Elizabeth against her bony chest. "Abide with me, sleep close, sweet dreams." And for a time Elizabeth becomes an infant like any other, though only for as long as it takes to gather the energy to recommence her violent objection to her father should I poke my head into the room.

I have taken steps to save my sanity. "I am going to London," I announced on a day when Elizabeth was particularly noisy. "I will no longer tolerate the tyranny of an infant who by rights should be spanked and put to bed in a room whose walls are thick enough to shut up the racket within."

"Mr. Bennet," answered Mrs. Bennet from her bed, "Elizabeth is but ten days old. It makes no sense to apply punishment suitable for a child much older, if then. You will simply have to put up with Elizabeth's temper until she can accommodate herself to our world. Sooner or later she will have to take nourishment from me and not from the bottle administered by Mrs. Rummidge. Sooner or later she will find comfort next to me and her sister, Jane, instead of the bony arms of Mrs. Rummidge, who I am beginning to suspect of being a fraud and a liar and no fit company for our children. Are you listening, Mr. Bennet?" There are times when deafness seems preferable to hearing such remonstrance, especially on those rare occasions when Mrs. Bennet approaches common sense. I remained silent. I planned my escape.

And now, dear reader, at the risk of seeming to complain in a most unmanly way, I must declare to this journal—and to myself—that the life of quiet contemplation, the life I had planned, has never come to fruition.

Bear with me. My aim, as I write, is to draw you to a closer understanding of this man whose world—through no fault of his own—is at present intolerable and shows no sign of easing. (Note the underscore.) With the achieving of my majority came the undeniable truth that my home and my garden and my woods and streams and the animals I imagined frolicking within were not mine. They would never be mine, not until the property is legally settled upon my son. Entailment is a curse, especially so with the heir apparent, my cousin, the insipid Collins, and his sycophantic ways. To think that this idiot might one day take his place at Longbourn kept me awake many a night, and so, early on, I took steps to lift that curse. The first was marriage.

Winnowing Mrs. Bennet out from all the girls keen to become my wife had not been an easy task, but at least until recently the result of my efforts, that being marriage, had not been particularly painful or inconvenient. Indeed, asserting my conjugal rights in the bedroom had proved not only convenient but pleasurable, reducing the necessity for trips into the village or to London to quiet the storms within me. Mrs. Bennet was comely; she was young and strong and not averse to my bedding of her. After the birth of Jane, she seemed agreeable to a certain amount of activity, even took occasional but undeniable enjoyment from my frequent forays into her bed. I quite enjoyed the flush in her cheek, her perfect little bosom, and the way her nipples retracted whenever I came near, though now as I think on it and on my somewhat limited experience, those nipples ought to have puckered out, not in. No matter. She could no more hide the pleasing curve of her waist than she could the suppleness of her limbs. Granted, she seemed to go to some trouble to cover herself; I had never seen so many bedclothes on one bed. But she could not help the dark curls that sprang from beneath her cap nor the shine in her dark blue eyes, sometimes tears, yes, but sometimes a ready spirit.

No matter, all that is behind me; for this wife of mine and her baby Elizabeth have ruined not only my present but my future. Such perfidy is beyond forgiveness. I will journey to London and pick up a book or two, and who knows what further adventures may come my way. After all, it is not my fault that things have not come out right. Besides, while London may be noisy it can offer nothing as unnerving as the eternal bawling and wailing from the bedroom above. In fact, I may find once more the man I was before this monumental betrayal. My sensibilities, many of them I recall as quite exquisite, may be restored.

As if to remind me of what I was fleeing, Mrs. Rummidge stood at the head of the stairs and screeched, "Shame on you running off to the city of sin and corruption whilst your dear ones struggle to survive! I swear on my virginity the sainted Jesus will come looking for you!"

"Shhh," I heard another voice, unmistakably my wife's,

say. "Let him go. You cannot miss what you did not want in the first place."

I slammed the door on my way out. "I have married a shrew," I muttered, "and she just seventeen."

On my way down the walk I began to whistle, a tune recalled from my youth, "Constant Billy."

Ch. 4

November at Longbourn

Dear Sister,

He has departed the scene, though not, alas, forever. He has gone to London, he says to purchase a book, though I know better. I did not come to this marriage completely ignorant of the ways of men. Do you recall Mindy Sharpton, she being left an orphan at an early age and forced to find her own way in the village? Did we not feel sorry for her even after we discovered her and the tailor's boy, Billy Cummings, locked in a tussle in the alley behind the shop? We hastened on but no detail had escaped us, not the frayed hem of her petticoat, not the mud on the soles of her boots, nor Billy's trousers around his ankles, nor the sickening sight of his mouth stretched into a rictus the likes of which we hoped never to see again. (Little did I know that I would too soon see just such a sight, and in my marriage bed at that!) Poor Mindy Sharpton with only one path left to her, and that trodden by men of the village whose respectability was unquestioned. I remember asking dear Mother why a man, Mr. Broadley the leather merchant, a husband and father, would seek out the company of a girl like Mindy Sharpton. Mother stiffened. "Now, young lady," she said, "leave well enough alone. It is the way of all men and has ever been such." We knew better than to persist with our questions and so, with a shrug, we grew further and faster into the womanhood that was our fate.

Am I not a Mindy Sharpton? Am I not a foolish girl who cast propriety to the winds and fell head over heels into the arms of a stranger? You might well ask, dear sister. You never ever called my behaviour into question; you never ever scolded me. You simply put your arms around me there in the little bedchamber in the house of our childhood and held me safe. "Hush, dear Marianne," you said over and over and smoothed my hair. What else you could have said I cannot imagine. Surely you were as ignorant as I of a future with a child and without a husband. Surely you were almost as frightened as I. The two of us—you and I—shared a desperation unknown to respectable young ladies, ladies like those Mother predicted her daughters would become. I betrayed her as only a daughter can betray a mother. Had she lived she would have known the shame of my indecency. She would have seen me as less than Mindy Sharpton, for after all, I did not have poverty to excuse my behaviour; I did not need to exchange my skirts for coin; I did not need to become a whore; and yet in her eyes I did. Illness is never a blessing, but in this instance it carried her off and saved her. But nothing saved me.

There are times when shame for the deceit with which I entered this marriage threatens to overwhelm me. But then, I look to my little Jane and wish with all my heart that Mother could be here to love her. All would be made right again . . . and . . . So Mr. Bennet travels to London to embellish his library? Of course he does. If indeed he does purchase a book I know what its subject will be, for I have seen what rests on his library shelves, hidden behind the volumes of birds and beasts he boasts of. "Ah, my dear," he has exclaimed more than once, "how much we have to learn from the world about us! The birds, do they not make you wonder how such flight is possible?" I am to look at him in admiration, impressed by his wisdom and intelligence. I am to be grateful for his attention. I am to look on him as my superior. "I urge you, my dear wife, to prepare yourself for the motherhood that awaits. Pray, leave off your contrariness and heed my counsel. It is certain that your mood would improve, as would the well-being of our children, especially that of my sons. We must look to the future." Tra-la, I want to say, I prefer the past.

And then came Elizabeth and with her the blame that fell upon me. He thought to comfort me: "I am not blaming you," he said, and added, "but it is your fault." Elizabeth and I are the reason Mr. Bennet is making his way to London. If he thinks to punish me by his absence I am content to have him think so inasmuch as his departure recalls a bit of the freedom I felt as a girl, before Mr. Bennet showed himself on my horizon, and returns to me some of the joy I felt in the company of my dear colonel. Such happiness must have showed itself at once because Mr. Bennet was no more out of the door than Mrs. Rummidge said, "O ma'am, your cheeks are rosy! I have not seen their colour since little Elizabeth came to us." Mrs. Rummidge at this moment held the baby in her arms as she does during most of her waking hours, quieting Elizabeth by way of some mystical spell I know not of. I am grateful to the woman, no matter that my daughter may be becoming bewitched; she is at least quiet. My strength is returning, as is the colour in my cheeks, as is my desire to see what lies beyond the upstairs chamber of my lying-in. Little Jane, sweet and compliant in her crib, babbles a bit and waves her little fingers in my direction; she takes my milk hungrily and often; she grows plump and rosy, just like her mother, and soon she will walk on her own. She is nothing like her little sister, although, given the difference in fathers, one ought not be surprised.

And so I am left to amuse myself and, dear sister, I am doing so though not as my husband would wish. In his absence I can return to *Pamela*. Alas, her misfortunes multiply with each page, caused by her Master, who pursues her unceasingly. Do you wonder at my affinity for this poor child? I will say, however, that her Master, unlike mine, brings her beautiful clothes: a silk nightgown, silken petticoats, laced shoes, Holland linen, and fine stockings, even a swan-skin undercoat. Good girl that she is, she refuses them and sews for herself flannel undercoats and rough shifts. Now, were Mr. B. to offer me fine silken garments, I would never for a moment refuse them, though of course, unlike Pamela, I am a married woman whose virtue belongs to the past. I shall add one additional difference between Pamela's Master and mine: Pamela's is handsome though nonetheless loathsome in his pursuit of this virginal girl. Oh, what luxury it is for me to while away the hours when I am detached from my babes amidst the pages of Mr. Richardson's novel.

But it is not just Pamela who provides my amusement. A unique sort of amusement comes from the slim volumes hidden on Mr. B.'s library shelves whose pages, as thin as the skin of onions, detail females like Mindy Sharpton in congress with men who resemble, dare I say, Mr. Bennet. So many and such varying ways of securing male pleasure I find astounding. I pray you will not think me too immodest, dear Jane, but I have no one else, certainly not Mrs. Rummidge, with whom to share my discoveries. I pray that you do not scold me for what I write: The drawings show figures whose outlines are smudged by fingers certainly not mine; they are upside and down, the male one way, the female the other, the female atop the male, sitting, lying, and she even standing with the male behind. Now, how is such discomfort supposed to pleasure him? Well, I will have ample time, with Mr. Bennet away, to reach an understanding of such positions. He thinks me lacking in curiosity? If only he knew how well versed I am in the world about him.

The rector and I will christen Elizabeth without her father's help, then. I will not expect either you or your fine husband, Mr. Phillips, to be on hand this time. It was so good of you both to make the arduous journey to Longbourn for little Jane's christening during that storm-tossed season. The snow seemed deeper than at any winter within memory, even Mr. Bennet said so, and the winds chilled us to the bone. The memory of Mr. Phillips's cough remains with me to this day. Your calm presence proved a balm to everyone, even to Mr. Bennet, whose disappointment over little Jane's sex he could not hide. I must say that had you been able to be present at Elizabeth's birth your calm demeanour might have prevented such violent outbursts as we were subjected to, not to mention his stomping from the house, shouting that he would make his way to London. Then again, I will confess to a certain relief brought about by his absence. Dear sister, I shall seek forgiveness in the next world; in this one I will seize what happiness I can. Allow me, while memory sharpens experience, to share with you what I call the Coming of Elizabeth:

A little less than one year had passed since Jane, and again the winds were fierce, a fitting storm for the birth of one who for nine months had been obstinate in my womb. Even Mrs. Rummidge, who insisted on boiling water well in advance of my delivery, agreed that this little one was no Jane and that indeed we had best begin the choosing of names for him.

Anticipating a son and despite my protestations, Mr. Bennet insisted on the presence of a doctor. A midwife and Mrs. Rummidge's hot water had done very well during my first labour with Jane, but Mr. Bennet would have none of it this time. He went so far as to import a Dr. Smellie from London to watch over me the moment my water broke. I must tell you, even in my pain, a more formidable figure I never saw and hope never to see again. Like a thundercloud, the doctor banged into my chamber, cape flying, hat clamped atop his head, clutching a leather satchel, which I took to hold his habiliments but which instead held the tools of his trade, among them that new invention, the forceps. I gasped at the sight—like tongs Cook uses to turn the sausages, only larger—and wondered aloud how it might be used. "The infant is occasionally reluctant to join us," he answered. "This will clasp his head and help him into his new life. Normally only a slight tug is necessary." His smile revealed a monstrous number of yellow teeth. Silently I prayed that my baby would come willingly. So, too, did the midwife who stood nearby and Mrs. Rummidge, who prayed, too, loudly, spilling hot water as she did.

But my baby did not come willingly. It seemed as if she

would not come at all. It seemed that she preferred to kick and stir and turn about within me, causing me endless pain. She did not wish to come out, nor did it seem that she wished to stay in. She was furious with her dilemma and I the object of her anger. At one minute I thought that my back would break in two and at another that my lower parts would give way altogether. Such pain, like bolts of lightning, came, then went, always to return with greater and greater violence and with greater frequency. The struggling of the child to be born seemed never to end and I cried out for my mother often. Even the midwife, who was surely accustomed to such goings-on, looked stricken. As for Mrs. Rummidge, her bucket was almost empty.

"Put that water down, old woman," Dr. Smellie ordered. "This is not the middle ages. You there," he said to the midwife, "pay attention; you are about to witness the most advanced methods of birthing. But first"—and his yellow teeth loomed large—"we must get you quiet." With that Dr. Smellie produced from his satchel some vials. Soaking a cloth with a tincture of something smelling so sweet as to sicken me, he showed his yellow teeth at me and said, "Place this cloth over your nose and mouth. Breathe deeply and your pain will be as nothing." I did as he asked and indeed, the pain receded. But so then did my baby and for a time it lay still. I drifted off and woke to see that everyone was a-slumber. The midwife lay curled at the foot of my bed, Dr. Smellie on the couch nearby, Mrs.

Rummidge on the bedclothes, which my exertions had pushed to the floor.

Mr. Bennet, you can assume, was nowhere to be found, though in my hazy half-consciousness I imagined I heard the clump of his boots as he paced back and forth along the hallway. Time lost its meaning. Awake, I was wracked with pain; surely something in me would burst from the kicking. I breathed from Dr. Smellie's cloth and once more fell asleep. This went on, said the midwife, who bless her heart refused to leave me, for a day and a night. "And that Dr. Smellie," she told me after, "made as if to depart, so impatient was he with you. And then you cried out, 'O Doctor, help my baby to be born!' To that he thundered, 'Push it out, woman, so that my forceps can grasp the head.'" I felt the forceps close to my nether region, which felt to me now quite distended. "Oh, please, sir," said the midwife, "might it not be possible for that instrument to harm the child? Might it not misshape the head, that so delicate part of a newborn?" "Quiet, woman," said Dr. Smellie, and I felt the cold metal upon me. Quickly, the midwife moved beneath his arm, came close to me, and whispered, "I believe you are quite wide enough for the baby to come through. One more push, dear child." I did as I was told and, suddenly, there she was, a caul hiding the red fuzz we would see anon. And there stood Dr. Smellie, forceps dangling uselessly from his hand. His grimace became a scowl as Mrs. Rummidge jumped up and down and sang merrily and of course loudly, "A caul! She is born with a caul! Good luck will follow her all of her life."

It was at this moment that Mr. Bennet chose to enter my bedchamber. "A what?" he demanded. "A caul? My son with a scummy cap on his head?!" And he ran out and down the stairs no doubt to his library to find what information he could about cauls. But not even halfway down the stairs he stopped and roared up, "She?! It's a she?!"

I have not seen him since. Nor have I seen Dr. Smellie, although the midwife told me not long ago that the good doctor was being investigated for possible burking, that being the murder of patients for purposes of obtaining corpses for medical research. Goodness gracious, who would think that so horrible a crime could happen in this day and age. Thank goodness. I suspect that Elizabeth, in all her infancy, chose to brave the elements of her new world on her own terms; thus was the forceps saved for another day. I shudder to think of it. I know only that it will not see my bedchamber again.

It seems so long ago and so much has happened since you braved the elements to join us in the rectory where the Reverend Brown dedicated Jane to God and asked for His guidance and protection of so little a child. You brought your very special Christmas cake and Mr. Bennet even opened a bottle of his precious port. We toasted Jane and each other, and for a brief time Mr. Bennet seemed happy and content. His forehead smoothed itself and his lips curled into a tiny smile and I saw him look upon his first-born with something akin to love. Would that he could do so for Elizabeth. Or me. Perhaps London will bring roses to his cheek, too.

I must now confess to you, dear sister. It is not just my babies' good health and, with the exception of Elizabeth's nightly tantrums, their good spirits that have returned the colour to my cheeks. It is news brought to me by none other than Mrs. Rummidge that a certain officer, recently returned from France, has taken a house in this very county! Could it be that same colonel I once knew and loved and whose most beautiful little daughter rests upon my breast even now? Of course, there must be many officers but somehow I do not think that many of them would seek to find a house so near my own. I have sent Mrs. Rummidge to find out his name. She has taken Elizabeth with her, thus providing me the time to write you such a long, long letter. My cheeks burn.

Your affectionate and loving sister,
Marianne

Ch. 5

In Which I Visit London

Cum morosa vago singultiet inguine vena.

"When you are tormented with fierce desire,
satisfy it with the first person that presents herself."

—PERSIUS

I will recount herein certain events and occurrences that surely will shock those who read this entry. However, I am determined to adhere to truthfulness, and besides, I shall be long gone when once this diary is unearthed. As for myself, I record these events in the hope that doing so will serve as a reminder that certain experiences need not be sought out even once, that unhappy results of happy coincidences may befall even the most upstanding among us, that the search for pleasure can very likely land one in the ditch. In short, take heed of what I write here. It is a warning to those as yet untried and a reminder for those who have been tried and seek to make their lives less wanting.

You who read this no doubt know me for the bibliophile that I am. Indeed, my happiest days were spent in my library among the books that for me were the stuff of life. And because you may have thought me a man of some learning, you will be surprised to learn that, as a scholar, I am a disappointed man.

In my youth I had been a lover of the classics, of theatre, and of—O truth, stay close!—brothels. At one time I considered myself something of a Renaissance man, though for how long I could maintain such an estimable title I could not conjure, there being no one at Longbourn to fan the flames of learning. Women and children are apt to douse all fires not of their own making. And so, before all my embers go out, I will travel to London in the hope of re-igniting some or all of them, then return home for another long cold winter, made colder by the reality of not one daughter but two.

Life at Longbourn has dampened my ardour for all that had been promised in my school years at Grandison's. Duty has prevailed over courage, habit over adventure. I will turn thirty this year. The world looks bleak. London beckons. I nod yes.

Ah, London, I had forgotten its assault on one's senses: it was all I could do to prevent myself from placing my handkerchief over my nose and mouth. I stumbled on a cobblestone, jerking myself awake to my surroundings. The noise of the crowds and the smell of open fires, the roasting meat, the calls from vendors to buy their wares, the waste both human and animal, all was as it had been during my boyhood years at the school not far from where I stood at this very moment. Human and animal excrement was familiar to me; after all, my own manor was surrounded by fields, and the barns of animals came close to my house. But I had not been in London for more than two years and now I felt disoriented, full of a nameless anxiety that made me an easy target for the pickpockets and thieves that roamed the streets. Here the smoke and the smells threatened the very air I took for granted in the country, though, as I would soon discover, London had not changed so very much since my days at school.

As a boy at Grandison's my mission had been to survive the seemingly endless cruelties of the masters and my schoolmates; I was but a country lad and a target for humiliation then as I was now, though not, in the former case, by women, who seem to have the upper hand in my present life. At school, Master Winthrop changed all that. Master Winthrop, steeped so far in Latin as to be blind and deaf to events past A.D. 42, and certainly to the life of a boys' school in the all-too-modern world of London, shimmered with his love of the language. Each term, when he came in his text to *Gallia est omnis divisa in partes tres*, Master Winthrop seemed to dance. When he conjugated—*cogito, cogitare, cogitavi, cogitatus*—he waltzed. When he declined—*fortuna, fortunae, fortunae, fortunam*—he did a little jig, and always he invited his students to join him. "Step lively, boys," he was heard to say, knowing full well that the boys would remain seated, slouched in boredom, gazing out the window where the playing fields offered relief from the tedium of Latin. I alone accepted his offer, and from that day forward the ridicule of the boys, the cane of the headmaster upon my backside ceased to trouble me. I had found my place. For four years with Master Winthrop the music never stopped. I began to have thoughts of Oxford and Cambridge.

However, not one for conversation or much of anything else in the English language, Master Winthrop could not provide me with an ease in society. I did not learn much at all in the way of conversing, except as I could say it in Latin, and so on those occasions when he, tired of my pestering, dismissed me, I turned to silence as my friend. Cicero's *Minus solum quam cum solus esset*—"Never less alone than when alone"—became mine and I was happy. Perhaps it was my solitude, my unwillingness to join in on the games and the pranks that boys at Grandison's found so exhilarating; whatever the reason, I remained on the edges of the school and went unnoticed by anyone who might have become a mentor. My father, albeit well-meaning and well-read, was not a rich man. My years at school had been a drain on his resources, and it came clear to me in my fourth year that monies for Oxford or Cambridge would not be forthcoming. So I returned to Longbourn, where no one spoke Latin, and to my father's fledgling library, at seventeen a disappointed man. Not long after, my father died, and too soon after that, my mother.

Over the years at Longbourn I felt myself rusting. My marriage, coming as it did on the other side of youthfulness, kept a few of my wheels up and running, although, were I forced to admit it, neither marital bliss nor even much satisfaction had been mine. Mrs. Bennet's initial reluctance and eventual passivity had turned the act of joy into something less, not that I would ever abjure my responsibility to beget a son and heir but that I had anticipated a bit of fun in the bargain. And so, in its absence, I felt nary a twinge of guilt when I decided to look beyond the bedclothes of my wife—yes, your mother, should the reader of this account be my son—to the city where experiences of every kind were to be had. Where but in London?

So you find me, in this year of 1786, on a mission. It is twofold: first and foremost to collect the book I had ordered from Clark's, my bookseller, and two, to take the pleasure due me from a lady of the evening. No talking required there.

Dear reader, what follows here is from memory and forces me to revisit humiliations past and present. So forgive me for what I am about to do. I must write about my travails as if they were happening to someone else. I will write about myself as another person, distant from the person I am now, and therefore less harmful to my constitution. Let him be known henceforth as Edward. He is an honest and clear-eyed young man through whose eyes we shall see circumstances as they happened. I shall wipe my dampened brow and join you posthaste. To horse!

Edward, His Story

Edward had had enough of virgins. His wishes ran now to a girl tried if not true, and so he arrived at Mrs. Brown's house, secure that he would be welcome, for he had visited in times past, the first when he was but a boy at Grandison's and a kinder head boy had taken him in hand and led him here where in short order he became a man. Since then, with each visit, Mrs. Brown's had become a destination where he found warmth and satisfaction. He felt in his pocket for his sheath, his friend and protector against diseases of the flesh. He looked forward to its use.

The front parlour was as it had been: two pier mirrors and a buffet with several plates of cold meats and mustards, fruits and cheeses, two chairs too stiff for sitting in for long. Mrs. Brown herself came forward. "Ah, good sir, I see you have returned to us. It has been too long." She offered a small plate of savouries—anchovies on toast—which he declined with a smile. "Yes, indeed," he answered her. "It is with pleasure I put myself in your care. You have never disappointed me."

Mrs. Brown smiled and smoothed her hands along the silk of her gown. Her bosom, which threatened to spill over the neckline, showed that, while Mrs. Brown was not old, neither was she young. She was, in the parlance of an earlier time, a beldam, perhaps even a grandmother. "I have someone in mind for you," she said. "I have just hired a young woman to look after my linen. She is quite lovely and as yet unused. I charge you to treat her with respect for I have great plans for her and do not wish to frighten her off." For a brief moment, as he gazed at Mrs. Brown, Edward wondered if at some point in his life he would find himself missing as many teeth as the beldam who stood before him. He tried not to stare. He pulled himself up and said, "I thank you, madam, but my request is different this time. Have you someone, someone like Bella who was my friend during my last visit, someone accustomed to the profession?"

"Bella is no longer with us," said Mrs. Brown, frowning, then brightening. "But I can offer you Martha, perhaps our most experienced girl yet charming in her own right. May I summon her?"

Martha appeared, pretty and well-mannered. With a smile she extended a hand and led him to her room above. Edward was optimistic.

Alas, his best-laid plans did not bear fruit. His sheath, so ready at hand, never left his pocket for Mr. Bennet could offer nothing that could be sheathed. Despite Martha's teasing of his hair and prolonged chafing of his member, despite the cordials she insisted he drink, despite all her efforts and his, he remained unmoved. "Let us rest a while," said Martha. "Your journey has tired you. Surely so fine a man as yourself will rise to the occasion in due time." But his enthusiasm dimmed as his capacity diminished. The time for striking was past; the iron never got hot and Edward took leave of Mrs. Brown's establishment with a woeful frown and a heavy heart.

He paid little attention to where he was going and before he knew it he found himself in Drury Lane where a signboard proclaimed "Sarah Siddons *is* Juliet in Shakespeare's Romeo & Juliet." He would rather it had read "Sarah Siddons *is* Lady Macbeth," a most rewarding play when last he read it in his library at Longbourn. Nonetheless, he bought a ticket. So far his journey to London—the vacation intended to ease his disappointment in his wife and his worries over the entailment and most of all his boredom with his life—was an utter failure. Perhaps this play, first encountered when he was a boy at Grandison's and thus mostly ignored, would provide at least a distraction. The Prologue promised "two hours' traffic of our stage," not long enough to purge his mood but short enough to keep him awake and perhaps restore his memory of how the play ended. The price of admission, two shillings, allowed him a seat in the first gallery; for a lesser amount he could have sat on the benches in the pit, where scholars, critics, and ladies of prey seated themselves. But he was not a scholar and he had had enough of women for hire, and the boxes at five shillings were beyond his pocket and his class. At two shillings, the first gallery was his due, as was a bit of Shakespeare. After all, what reason did he have to be in this great city save to capture what pleasures might arise or, in his case, he thought sadly, did not rise. Perhaps this play would surprise him as it had not in his youth. "Two households, both alike in dignity . . ." intoned the Chorus. So far so good.

Not long into Act I Edward realized that this was a play about man's sexual fortitude and focused his attention on Romeo. Here was this whippersnapper, the estimable John Kemble would have us believe, rampaging about the stage because some girl he barely knew refused to lift her skirts for him. "She hath forsworn to love," Romeo bleats. Edward considered leaving early. But then comes Juliet, who it seems is thirteen years old and who will be married soon to County Paris. Ye gods, thought Edward, she is Mrs. Bennet's age almost, though almost twice as tall, taller than Mr. Kean. He sighed and thought, And soon Juliet will have a child, probably a girl, just as Mrs. Bennet had, and nothing good can come of this play. He did, however, decide to see it through. Will Juliet complain and refuse the County Paris? Will Romeo take matters into his own hands? Will Edward see his own domestic tragedy enacted before his very eyes?

"Under love's heavy burden do I sink," says Romeo. Edward shifted in his seat, impatient with the melodrama over a girl the boy had never laid a hand to. The lady in the seat next to him shifted, too, it seemed to Edward, away from him. From the stage Romeo sulks over love: "It is too rough, / Too rude, too boist'rous, and it pricks like thorn." His friend Mercutio speaks sense to him: "If love be rough for you, be rough with love." Now, that I understand, thought Edward, relaxing into the cushions. We'll just see if Romeo has the good sense to heed good advice. But no. Unsuccessful in his drive to unseat Rosaline from her virginity, he simply turns his efforts into tossing up Juliet. Unfair, simply unfair that this scarcely more than a boy gets all these chances. Edward crossed his arms over his chest, touching slightly the elbow of the lady who sat next to him. "I beg your pardon," he whispered. She smiled a polite forgiveness, her downward glance pricking him in the same place as Romeo's. Alas, it seems that neither he nor the young hero onstage is to find satisfaction: "O, wilt thou leave me so unsatisfied?" Edward leaned forward in his seat. So did the lady next to him.

Well, by the holy rood, if Juliet doesn't come across! And willingly, passionately, and gloriously! And so soon, it's only Act II! Romeo leaves off his adolescent maunderings and settles down to loving. "Sleep dwell upon thine eyes, peace in thy breast!" Edward capitulated. He, too, felt great stirrings—and knew at once that they would come to naught.

In fact, they came to worse than naught, they came to the end of love and life and of the play, and, when the lady next to him rose to leave with her escort, the end of possibility. Edward was moved beyond words or movement and remained in his seat until the theatre had emptied itself of all but those even more forlorn than he, the cleaning women. "A glooming peace this morning with it brings. The sun, for sorrow, will not show his head."

And now, dear reader, the worst is over and I can resume my role as self-confessor and teller of my tale. The sun did show its head, as so far in its history it does, and the following morning dawned as brightly as it was possible to dawn through the fog- and smoke-streaked window of my chamber. I sprang from my bed, the gloom of the previous evening dispelled by the promise of what this day would bring. This was the day I would call on Mr. Clark, bookseller, and by day's end be the proud owner of Burton's *Anatomy of Melancholy*.

I had been waiting to own this book for the entirety of my reading life. And now, if Arnold Clark's message held up, that very book awaited me at the shop. "It is the fifth edition," Clark had warned, "not the first, but it is in fine shape for one that is more than a hundred years old. I think you will be pleased."

I was pleased. Clark placed the volume in my hands, heavy from its almost 800 pages, bound in calf so Clark said, the title lettered on the spine in gold: *The Anatomy of Melancholy*. Very carefully I opened the book to a page that began, "Borage and Hellebore / Sovereign plants to purge the veins of melancholy and cheare the heart / of those black fumes which make it smart / To clear the Brain of misty fogs which dull our senses and Soul clogs / the best medicine that ere God made / for this malady, if well asseid."

I am not a religious man, as you no doubt know, but surely some spirit greater than my own had brought me to this book. The price was beyond what I had expected but I paid it readily and, tucking the volume safely beneath my waistcoat, I promised silently to purchase hellebore and borage, though their location remained unknown to me. "I bid you a fond farewell, Mr. Clark," I said, and with a smile I did not have when I entered, I exited into Covent Garden, warmed by what I held close. So great was my delight that I passed without noticing the cockfights and the dwarves and the puppet shows, the growing crowd, gaily drunk, on its way to another public hanging. The stench of London, the filth of the streets, the sight of raw sewage failed to trouble me even as the glow of the coal fires lit my way and hurried me on to the inn where, on my final night in this great city, I would lay down both book and head.

Covent Garden, rightly named Venus Square, was perfect for assignation, prolonged or spontaneous, its footpaths lined with girls, five or six of them, most dressed in genteel fashion. Taverns nearby were ready for those shy of taking their pleasure in the open air, but I paid little attention to the solicitations of the girls. I hugged my new companion to me, eager to return to my chamber where I could lay my very own book flat and read with my own eyes the wonders of Mr. Burton's cogitations.

Without having paid attention to where I was or where I was going, I found myself, at dusk, on Westminster Bridge, the Buildings of Parliament nearby, once the home of kings and princes grand and glorious. There in their shadow, leaning against the low wall of the bridge, elbows akimbo to afford a passerby full view of her ample bosom, a woman neither old nor young, neither beautiful nor ugly, smiled amiably at me. "What's your hurry, dearie?" I smiled back; indeed, I was in no particular hurry: my mission to London had been fulfilled, almost, and here with her dark hair blowing in the wind and her skirts raised to show easy entry, she looked to be the final piece. Pleased with my accomplishments so far and confident beyond measure, I drew near. She held out her hand, I dropped four shillings into it, her smile grew wider. "Name's Alice," she said, "if you like." In the growing darkness, to the sound of the Thames flowing below, I grew bold. In full command I ordered, "Raise them high." Alice's skirts billowed about us and with one thrust I found my mark and plunged. So great was my exertion and so pleasurable that I forgot that only the darkness obscured me from public view, I forgot that I had forgotten my sheath, I forgot that my most precious possession was about to fall from my waistcoat. But fall it did. "Ow!" cried Alice, and I looked down to see her foot crushed beneath all 732 pages of my *Anatomy*. At once I withdrew, but not soon enough, for alas, all that I had stored within came rushing forth and spent itself onto *Melancholy*. I fell to my knees, clutching my breeches about my naked haunches, and with my coat sleeve swiped at the cover of my beloved book. "Could have been worse," called Alice as she limped away. "Might've dropped into the water. I'd say you had a bit of luck there, dearie."

I had desecrated a sacred object and it wasn't Alice. It was time to leave this bridge, this city, and return to the country where I and my book might be restored to cleanliness and perhaps even a touch of godliness. The journey looked to be a long one.

And I, the present-day Mr. Bennet, am relieved that this tale is ended and that the moral therein will be heeded by those who come after.

Ch. 6

January at Longbourn

My dear sister!

How fierce this winter! The driving rain makes roads impassable and we are locked inside most of the day. I do so wish the weather had allowed a visit from you and Mr. Phillips; your company would have made Christmas here less dreary. The children are still too young to take part; Mr. Bennet is even more peevish on holidays if you can imagine and spends most of every day in his library with his recent acquisition, an enormous book with *Melancholy* etched upon its spine. He emerged only to tell me be sure and plant some hellebore, whatever that is. I was happy to see the end of the season.

But not all my news is doleful, for there is to be a ball!

At the grandest house in the county and perhaps all of England! And the host and the man who has leased this fine establishment is none other than Colonel Millar! I hear he is retired from the guard and is to become a man of leisure, lord of Northfield in all its glory. The gardens alone make it a paradise! What shall I wear? I have nothing. I shall have to sew something. Thank goodness Mama stood over us all those years ensuring that our skill with the needle matched the manners she was equally insistent upon. And thank goodness the ball is not so near at hand. I shall have ample time to order fine silk and to turn it into something beautiful. Or perhaps I will seek Mr. Bennet's permission to engage the talents of Mrs. Salther, the seamstress in the village, whose reputation quite precedes her. He will of course refuse me as he does all my little requests. No matter. I shall not wear a cap at the ball even though married women do. I shall seek to appear as fresh and lovely as I was the day Colonel Millar made me his. I shall go capless and show a proper amount of my breasts, which are as creamy and pert as ever despite little Jane, who would tug them downward at every opportunity. Elizabeth of course apparently sees them not as the fount of life but as weapons against which she fights with her little fists and her surprisingly bellicose jaw. I would swear she was born with teeth.

And so, to save her from starving and me from throttling her, Elizabeth now lives with a wet nurse at the far end of the village. I visit her every week and often Mr.

Bennet joins me; he seems amused at his tiny red-headed vixen who tightens her little fists into balls of fury every time I come near. Truth be told, Mr. Bennet visits her more than once a week and without me. Clearly he favours the impossible Elizabeth over the sweetness of Jane. Perhaps he senses in her rage something akin to his own feelings. I shall never know because he does not confide in me any more than does Elizabeth. Both of them insist on going their own way, preferably without the one who is their wife and mother.

I have never sought to concern myself with Mr. Bennet's darker moods and where they might come from. If pressed, however, I would admit that he returns from his visits to this irrepressible little creature seemingly lighter in mind, often a tiny smile on his usually dour mien.

I must defend myself to you, dear sister, for my actions even though I am not the only mother to place her infant with a wet nurse. You who hoped for so long to become a mother yourself must wonder at my willingness to give over the nourishment of my child to a stranger. I, too, believed for many weeks that I was a failure as a mother even though little Jane seemed happy and content. But with Elizabeth's first breath, she would not take nourishment from me and believe me, dear sister, I tried until my nipples burned like fire and the milk ran dry even for my adored Jane. I had no alternative but to seek out another source of milk lest both my babies cease to grow. Strange as it may seem, once Elizabeth was settled with Mrs. Dugan, my milk began to flow again and Jane continued to thrive. Elizabeth herself grew fat and happy. Her howling gave way to gurgles and she was quite the wonderful baby, at least in my absence.

What is it that makes for enmity between those who should be close? What can it be in an infant that makes for such anger, for angry is how she appears to me. She seems furious with me, not with Mr. Bennet or Mrs. Rummidge, or now Mrs. Dugan. It is I who unleashes the squalling. No one, least of all I, understands where her rage comes from. Perhaps, I have wondered, she blames me for not feeding her properly. Perhaps she blames me for feeding Jane so happily. Perhaps she was simply born angry and I am her chosen target. We shall see. In the meantime, she will remain with Mrs. Dugan and I will peep in on her every so often. A quiet home is a blessing and so is Mrs. Dugan.

Indeed, "quiet" is the word for Mr. Bennet, though "absent" might be more to the point. He has not come near me since his return from London. Contrary to my expectations, he did not bring with him onion skin papers with ladies penned naked upon them. I know this because I scoured his library shelves and cupboards one day while he was seeing to the rents. Instead, everywhere in the house or out, he carries the large, heavy book called *Anatomy of Melancholy*. He is scarce seen without its company; he holds it close to his chest as he paces back and forth in his library as if to keep it safe or perhaps to draw from it whatever wondrous knowledge it holds. It is his constant companion and for that I am grateful. He no longer paws me or assaults me in my chamber or in the kitchen, not even in the barn loft, a place that leaves me with nothing but sneezes and itching in my most private parts.

Which is what Mr. Bennet does much of: itching. It is clear that he is uncomfortable. He cannot sit still for more than a few seconds without scootching about, without excusing himself from the parlour, from the dining table, from his bedchamber to which, dear sister, he repairs even before the evening candles are lit. Not at all as it was before he made his way to London, when he sought me out in my chamber, the pantry, the clothespress, even the dining room, beneath the sideboard, where he insisted no one would think to discover us. I prefer this present to the difficult past. I do, however, wonder at the cause of his discomfort and while I do not wish it to persist, I am grateful for the freedom it gives me in my daily life. I am free to wonder about Colonel Millar, free to imagine placing his daughter, my own Jane, into his arms, free to hope for rescue from my unhappiness. At the same time, I imagine that Colonel Millar will not come to his new home unaccompanied. If I allow myself to do so, I fret and stew over who she might be and what her position is. Wife? Sister? Bespoken? Common sense tells me that a man of his position and reputation and good looks would not remain single for long. What then, dear Marianne? I lie awake nights, alone (I thank the good lord for Mr. Bennet's itch), little Jane at my breast, aching for the colonel to come to his rightful place, beside me—or else to take me to my own rightful place, the magnificent Northfield. But then I scold myself, Oh, Mrs. Bennet, you are a married lady, a mother of two, this dreaming is such nonsense. And I answer, Oh, Mrs. Bennet, you are seventeen and ought not to wear a cap at all.

I cannot wait for the spring. I cannot wait for the silk that will be my gown, the laces that will trim its bodice and its neckline. My dear sister, would you consider lending me your pelisse in case the spring is more cruel than I anticipate?

Affctly,
Your loving sister

Postscript: Mr. Richardson's Pamela has been carried away to a far-off estate where she is watched over by the odious Mrs. Jewkes! What will befall her? Nothing good, I expect.

Ch. 7

In Which I Fall Victim to My Folly (and Rightly So)

"Evils have their life and limits,
their diseases and their recovery."

—MONTAIGNE

I was no longer melancholy. I was burning in hell. I had not slept a night through since my return from London. I had not sat at table for the entirety of a meal. I could not sit for more than a single moment with my books in my library without feeling the fires of my inconstancy, of my thoughtless and momentary lustfulness, of my failure to protect myself and my own anatomie from the hideous mites that had clawed their way into my groin and showed every intention of remaining, intent on burying their heads into the very life of me. That I knew the cause of my agony and the name for it gave me no ease whatsoever. What mattered now was to find the remedy.

I did not know of a remedy. Not one of my books addressed the matter of crabs. I could scarcely enquire of the servants; already they looked at me suspiciously, and Cook, for one, had forbidden me entry into her kitchen. "What with the two little ones and such illness about," she said, "I must ensure that all surfaces of my kitchen are kept clean and polished. You had best keep away, sir, at least until the children are older." I knew what she really meant, that my rubbing myself up and down every door jamb, my grinding against every counter edge, spelled disease or at the very least was so disturbing to witness that barring me from her premises seemed the only reasonable course.

Forbidden, too, was the child who had become my beloved Elizabeth. The mere thought of the mites infesting her tiny body was enough to keep me from the path to the cottage of her wet nurse. I no longer wandered alone down that path where my beloved daughter awaited my cooing and petting and bundling, away from the criticisms of those to whom my behaviour would appear unmanly. I no longer accompanied Mrs. Bennet on her weekly visits, much to her consternation. "But Mr. Bennet," she exclaimed, "you showed such promising signs of fatherhood, how is it that suddenly you choose to ignore her!" I could only growl, satisfying neither of us.

I growled because I was not accustomed to speaking aloud, especially in defense of myself. At Grandison's, with the exception of conversation in Latin with Master Winthrop, I found no use for speaking. The boys spoke to each other and, in the din of their own sounds, to the halls and the walls of the school. No one spoke to me and so I became comfortable with silence. My books spoke to me and, in a most vibrant way, I answered them.

Women, however, were not books; they spoke at once and they spoke back and they seemed to speak all day and into the night. "I'm sure you're right, my dear," became my conversational companion and, most of the time, served to soothe Mrs. Bennet's occasional flare-ups. These days I rarely contradicted her or insisted on examining her opinions or demands. So when she tossed her curls at dinner and announced, "I have changed my plans. I will have Mrs. Salther in the village make my ball gown. I am much too busy, and she has a fine reputation," I nodded and said, "I'm sure you're right, my dear." She looked at me querulously, unconvinced by my ready response, and said, "Are you a friend to good health, Mr. Bennet?" Such had been my behaviour of late—all the rubbing of my lower parts she could not help but notice—that my willingness to consent to her every request she found suspect. To her question, I nodded a yes and added, "my dear." I rose from the table to "see to matters in the fields" and hurried out.

I noted that Mrs. Bennet frowned, but only for a moment, for now, with my permission, she would send a note to Mrs. Salther announcing a visit within the week.

I found something akin to conversation in the person of Tom Watkins, one of my tenant farmers. I had on occasion stopped by to watch this man of strong body and sensible mind as he gathered hay, washed out the hog slop, scrubbed down the walls of the creamery. Every so often, I would growl as befitted a landlord, "Fine weather we're having, Tom." Tom would stop whatever he was doing and answer, "Indeed it is, sir." "Any difficulties with the animals, Tom?" I would enquire. Then Tom would list and explain problems with calving, with binding the sheaves, with warming the chickens. Never did he complain about his own circumstances or those of his large family. With a healthy wife, three boys, and two girls, he seemed a contented man; to be sure, he was an enviable man. And so I was hopeful, nay, desperate, that I could find a remedy for my condition by way of Tom, for surely Tom, with his sheep a-graze in the common lands and his wheat fields alive with all manner of creepy-crawly beasties, would have knowledge of what to do when these mites got out of hand and into the trousers of even so genteel a landholder as myself. I pulled on my galoshes and plunged out onto the muddy path which would lead me to relief from suffering.

"Mud, sir," said Tom, pulling on his forelock. "I've heard that mud or, better yet, fat from a duck packed upon the place will smother the little bastards, if you'll forgive my forwardness, sir. That and ash."

"Ash?"

"Ash from the grate, sir."

Ah, simple enough.

"My wife uses mud or if there is no mud, such as in the cold weather, chicken fat, duck being beyond our means. She makes it into a paste with the ash and before you know it the children's head lice are on the run."

I explained to Tom that the remedy was for his sheep-herders who had complained of discomfort. "Ah yes," said Tom, "sheep are lousy beasts."

I thanked Tom and strode back up the path until I came to a copse. I bent down and began to scratch at the earth until I extracted not what one would call mud but what looked to be a sufficient amount of earth for application to the affected area. Holding it in my left hand, I tugged at my breeches with my right until the affected area was liberated to the air. Carefully, I smoothed the dirt upon myself and then more onto my parts of honour and felt at once a diminishing of the prickling that had been my constant companion for these past weeks. The problem now arose of what to do next, what with my nether region covered with flakes of earth. I decided to sit beneath the grove, now leafless in this late winter, until the dirt had caked itself upon me and I could continue on my way with minimal damage to my linens. I breathed deep sighs of relief. I was at peace.

(And may I say here, in this journal, that I am relieved that only my male heirs will read this.)

"Drat!" I exclaimed, for here came Mathilda, the most comely daughter of Tom, switching the cow that would provide her infant brothers their milk. She had no business being here, for she and the cow belonged in the common field some distance away, not here so close to the home farm and to her landlord whose breeches encircled his ankles and whose bare bum was on view. Hastily I covered myself with my waistcoat, then struggled to hide behind the largest tree, trailing shards of earth, now mostly dried, and my breeches behind me.

Mathilda, to whom the sight of bare bums was most likely a daily occurrence and whose brothers rarely donned breeches, passed by, heedless of her landlord's humiliation. She hummed prettily as she strolled, flicking the backside of the cow as she went, and, as she passed that same landlord, hiding himself behind the tree, she sang, "As Nell sat underneath her cow, upon a cock of hay, brisk John was coming from the plough, and chanc'd to pass that way." My erection tossed away most of what earth remained, leaving me once again naked as a jay although this time with no Martha, no Mrs. Bennet, no anyone to provide release. The pain of the crabs gave way to the pain of passion unspent and I slumped to the ground, relieved to see Mathilda disappearing into the distance.

Why, I wondered, was my every effort to exercise my God-given right met with humiliation and despair and now disease. It did not seem fair. Even my encounters with my wife, lawful as they were, left me unsatisfied, albeit spent. Something was missing. My few forays into Mrs. Brown's brothel had afforded release but no real pleasure. My few years as a husband had brought with them a cold and withholding wife. And my most recent adventure, if that was what one could call it, with the doxy Alice had left me with nothing but suffering and shame. As I thought back on my life as a sexual man, I decided I had never been one. I groaned as I thought of the evening ahead, my wife bent over her embroidery hoop, myself attempting to sit still long enough to read a chapter. Perhaps, though, the earth had done it; perhaps I would be allowed once again to luxuriate within the pages of my beloved books—and ultimately in the company of my adored Elizabeth.

I struggled up onto the path and slowly made my way home, if that was what one could call it. The itching had returned. Was there never to be an end to suffering?

Ch. 8

In Which I Suffer

Parque per omnes Tempestas.

"The tempest rages everywhere."

—VIRGIL

(Be warned herewith. This entry may repulse you e'en as it educates you.)

I struggled to pull my wife's fine-toothed comb through my pubic mound. Finally, one of her appurtenances was proving useful. I winced as I tugged but continued, for surely my exertions would at last free me from the dominion of these terrible beasties. The beasties, save for a few which fell to the floor, seemed content to remain where they were and quite able to escape the enemies advancing upon them. I would have to shave. A grisly affair.

I heard the footsteps of the maid. Here I was again, my breeches down around my ankles. What was it about women that brought about such degradation? The comb's teeth lay sprinkled about the floor, the handle still clenched in my hand. "What is it, Margaret?" I called impatiently.

"Madam has told me to come clean your room. She said it hadn't been done in ever so long. I tried to explain that you shooed me away every time I came near. But now she's having none of it. It wouldn't take but a moment; I shall be as quick as I can. Oh please, sir, Mrs. Bennet is on a tear. I've never seen her quite like this, so quick to anger, so easy to cry."

Now what was that about, I wondered. She was indeed more given over to moods than ever I recalled. I had to admit that, by and large, my wife was an even-tempered little thing, even cheery and forever insisting on what she called the sunshine of life rather than the gloom. With "gloom," she looked pointedly at me, who just as pointedly looked away. However, since my return from London she seemed to be on a rampage: energetic, laughing, running about, slamming doors, her behaviour not unlike little Jane's, who, not yet two, spent her days copying her mother though at times it seemed the other way round. But little Jane did not descend into equal parts sadness and despair with such moping about as her mother exhibited, such flopping into chairs, toying with her food but eating little, staring endlessly into the evening fire. This was a new Mrs. Bennet and I was just as happy that I had closeted myself, per necessity of course, because certainly her recent behaviour did not draw me to her side. Conjugal relations, at least for the present, were out of the question, so in all honesty, I saw no reason to seek her out. Not that I preferred picking nits or, as would happen shortly, shaving myself, but as frustrating as all this was, I saw signs of victory. Where my wife was concerned, I saw nothing that was in my power to do. A stalemate, that's what she was.

"Go away," I called to the maid. "Tell your mistress I will join her for dinner. Then you can tidy up here. Go on."

As the sound of her footsteps subsided I got out my razor strop and began to sharpen the last weapon in my arsenal.

From her bedchamber I could hear wailing, something about her figure ballooning, then tears, then remonstrating upon whatever her maid was doing. "Tighter!" I heard. "Pull harder!" Then a shriek, then the sound of a body collapsing, probably onto the bed, then tears again. And then clearly, "Mrs. Salther will have my head when next she fits me. She will scold me. She will tell me there is not enough silk in all of London to cover my outcroppings. Dear God, am I never to have a waist again? What use is motherhood if all it does is to make the mother bulge beyond reasonable restraint?" Stamping on the floor.

Despite this racket, I, who had had the forethought to soap myself thoroughly, propped the mirror against my footstool and, monitoring my progress in the glass, shaved calmly and carefully, not a nick but not a gnat, either, not one that I could see at any rate.

Apparently my wife had descended to the kitchen, from where she continued her complaints at an ear-splitting volume. This time it was Cook who felt the force of her fury. "What are you doing? I ordered the potato crusts to accompany the salmon. You know how the master enjoys those crusts! And here you seem to be putting together some kind of anchovy crisp. I am so disappointed in you, Nellie!"

"But, madam, when I went to make the gravy for the potatoes, the duck fat was missing. I cannot imagine where it might have gotten to. I shall look once more in the larder but I do not expect it will appear simply because I have come again to look for it."

"Ridiculous. Duck fat does not disappear. Someone has got hold of it. Someone has stolen it away. Though to what purpose I cannot think." I could hear the commencing of tears.

Nellie continued, "And my pastry cloths, they are disappeared, too, and so the apple tarts you planned cannot be achieved!" Nellie's tears commenced.

"Now my house is full of thieves!" cried Mrs. Bennet. "Is it not enough that I have to contend with corsets that won't shut and anchovies for supper and . . . most likely the absence of biscuits for the morning. It is too much!"

"Stop! Oh, please don't!" Nellie begged. "Not my tossing-pan!" The clang of pan against wall shook the house. And then another shattering, probably the mixing bowls, then two plops, hers, and then another's, this time, I suspected, atop Nellie's baking table. Sobs and sighs. The two of them made a duet of misery.

Upstairs, I smiled with satisfaction. I had almost completed my task; shortly I would be as smooth and as clean as a newborn babe. All I needed do now was to make the poultice according to Tom's instructions, apply it to the affected area, and bind it with Nellie's snowy white linens. Careful not to spill, I spooned the duck fat (1/2 C.) into Nellie's wooden bowl and added ash (2 T.) from the hearth. Mixing well with my left hand, I held my nose with my right, for the aroma was not at all pleasant, and looked out the window, for the grey greasy batch which lay reeking in the bowl did not recommend itself to viewing. Neither was it pleasant to dip my fingers into the bowl and apply the mixture to my now snowy lower half, but I did so quickly and as quickly wrapped Nellie's pastry cloths around and over the poultice. I felt instant relief. I counted myself cured: smelly but cured. All would be well.

Downstairs there was no poultice for what ailed Mrs. Bennet. "I am a barrel," she wept. "No one will look at me, let alone ask me to dance."

Nellie tried her best. "But, madam, you are only a year past birthing. It takes time, mum, for female parts to fall back into place. And you have such a lovely face," she added, desperate to provide comfort and save what was left of her kitchen.

"That's what they all say about fat women!" she sobbed, and collapsed onto the bread board. "I will starve myself," she said resolutely. "I will return to my former self. I will have a waist. I will! And then I will dance at the ball. Someone is sure to ask me, if only Mr. Bennet." Two floors above the ranting, I winced.

I had no intention whatsoever of attending the ball she was so eager to attend. I had heard of nothing but the ball ever since my return from my unfortuitous journey to London. Mrs. Bennet's current fatuousness, I supposed, was provoked by thoughts of what I considered one of the most useless gatherings of country society. Nothing was to be gained from attendance at such an event. A ball, it seemed to me, was merely a chance for the ladies of the county to dress in a provocative and foolish manner and either create gossip or gather it. Even for something as simple as an assembly on the village green, ladies would dine on it, have tea over it, dash off notes about it for months following. Imagine, and here I shuddered, the spillage into my daily life of something so grand as this ball to be held on the grand estate of the grand and mysterious Colonel Millar. Long ago I had learned to dance in order to secure a wife. Now I had one. I did not have to dance ever again. Nor would I, no matter how loudly and how long Mrs. Bennet's protestations continued. I suspected that the keening from the kitchen below was just a tune-up. I prepared myself for the worst.

First, though, I would pay a visit to Tom to thank him for his advice, which had had an immediate effect. I found him standing before his cottage holding his goose, dead of a broken neck. "For shame!" he cried angrily to a heaven as indifferent to him as it was to his goose. "That damnable hunt and look what it brings. This!" He turned to me. "You see what they have done, sir. I have lost six of my chickens and the vegetable plot will not render us our food this summer what with the trampling it has endured. I see no reason for such as they call it, a ritual."

I saw no reason for it, either. It had been assumed that, as a member of the landed gentry, I would join the others for the hunt when I reached my majority. But I had begged off, claiming a twisted ankle, then a wrenched thumb, a cold in the head, a misery in the gut, anything that would exempt me from what I considered a barbarity. No one I knew would agree with me, no one would sympathize with my view, but no one would dare call me a liar, either, and so my periodic objections were nodded over in sympathy until finally I was not bothered by invitations to run small animals to ground.

"I beg your pardon, sir," said Tom. "I do not mean to trouble you with my woes. You have caught me at an unfortunate time."

"Tom," I said, "I share your anger at the sporting life. Our new neighbor, this Colonel Somebody, is no doubt responsible for this latest insult. But there's nothing to be done. The hunt will go on long after you and I are gone." Still, I thought to myself, I can see to it that he does his damn hunting elsewhere, not on my land.

Tom nodded and stood quietly, wondering as to the cause of this unusual visit from me, at the same time eager to make the best of the goose that lay lifeless on the ground. He would have to bleed her and pluck her soon else she would turn unfit for supper.

I felt oddly embarrassed and did not meet his eye. "Tom," I said, "you have had this wife of yours for a goodly number of years, have you not?" Tom looked at me curiously. I persisted, "Have you found her to be, to be . . . companionable?"

"In what way, sir?" Tom answered.

I caught his smile and realized that I was providing him amusement rarely available on such a grand scale. Undaunted, I proceeded. "Has she been . . ." I paused, looking past Tom into the fields, which seemed so orderly, so productive, so unlike anything in my domestic life. "Has she been a good wife?"

"Aye, sir, she has." Apparently, Tom decided to fill in the space of my discomfort until I could bring myself to say what was truly on my mind. "She looks after the children, she is a passable cook, and now that our eldest is fifteen and able to look after the young ones, my wife is able to help me in the fields."

I could not hide my envy. Tom continued nonetheless. "I am pleased with her in every way. She is of course not the pretty little thing she was in the early years. Five children have had their way with both her face and her figure." I stared at Tom. Here at last was a man who understood me.

"Your boys came late, I believe," I said.

"To be sure," answered Tom. "We had quite given up on the notion of ever having sons. We were content with our two daughters and believed our time of begetting to be over." I nodded vigourously. "But then, nature being what it is," said Tom, "she grew big again and delivered one son and not long after another son and finally the babe you see there in the cradle. Three sons." Tom said this proudly. I forgave him his little preening. I must have appeared once more downcast. Tom seemed to know now what was troubling his landlord. "So I guess my advice to anyone, if of course it were asked for, would be to just keep trying. You never know with women. They surprise you from sunrise on." Then, taking a deep breath, he ventured: "If I may, sir, up there at the house"—he pointed to my domicile—"is what we down here in the cottages call a yeller."

"A what?"

"A yeller."

I considered what sort of reprimand was in order. "Explain yourself," I said.

Tom took a deep breath. "Well, sir, a yeller is someone, most always a woman, who yells." Tom looked as if he wished he had kept still but realized that it was too late now for silence. "The night air, in clear weather—sir, I mean no harm—carries sound that bad weather keeps at home." He hurried. "Down here, for instance, we hear the high-pitchedness of especially a woman's voice and when it has in it an urgency we are bound to listen."

I felt my face redden. "And what do you hear?"

Encouraged, Tom continued. "Well, sir, coming at night as it did, once we decided among us that this woman was not in danger, that the yelling was likely the accompaniment to an act of marriage, we judged it be a . . . a sort of protest."

"A protest?" I pretended, unsuccessfully, to ignorance.

"Well, sir, it was by no means the sound of contentment, 'twas more like anger, more like the cry of a mare who was being mistreated." He kept his eyes on the ground. "That's what we call a yeller, sir, since you asked."

I was confounded and fell into an awkward silence. Finally, I said, "And what would you do with a yeller? That is, if you wanted to end the yelling." I watched Tom's foot make circles in the dust.

"If it were mine, like the mare I just mentioned, I'd try to gentle her, try to get her to understand I meant her no harm. Could take a bit of time."

I raised my eyes. "You're a good man, Tom."

"If you say so, sir."

I felt a gentle wind cool across my brow. I felt the warmth of the sun. I noted the wren, the lark, a hawk.

Across the field, just on the other side of the wood, the stream ran fast. It was spring, the beginning of new life. I started for home, my groin healed and full of purpose. “See to your chores, Tom,” I said.

“Indeed I will, sir,” said Tom. Sophie would be pleased. Goose for dinner and it not even Christmas.

Ch. 9

April at Longbourn

Dear Sister,

I take this moment to pen my thoughts. Mr. Bennet is gone once more into the countryside as is his wont of late. In his absence, I secure myself in his library and take up once more Volume I, in which Pamela is nearly violated! It was with much fear that I approached those pages in which it would be determined whether or not Pamela's Master, with the help of the odious Mrs. Jewkes, would take her without her consent, destroying her virginity and defiling her purity. Depravity of this nature I have not seen, not in any barnyard, not in any book.

I have not time to describe the entirety of the trickery and deceit from which my heroine suffered because I am due for a fitting at Mrs. Salther's. I have decided that I will wear beneath my ball gown a corset which hooks in the front. With that, I can dress myself, at least my undergarmented self, without the disapproval of my maid, who would most surely blush when she saw the rise and thrust of her mistress's bosom. Seduction, though, is far from my thoughts; admiration is what I seek, not of the guests at the ball, but of Colonel Millar, the possessor of my heart and of Northfield, the grandest estate in the county. To that end, something will have to be done with my unruly curls as I am determined not to wear a cap. Dear sister, can you advise me?

And now I must turn back to the library for a visit with Pamela. O la! Seduction of a not very gentlemanly kind seems to await our heroine. I will confess that I read on with avidity.

Imagine this! That to gain Pamela's trust and entry into her bed her lord and master dressed himself as a woman! I cannot imagine Mr. Bennet cooking up any such charade, although my purity has not been at issue for quite some time, thank you very much. Another difference is that her admirer seems dotty from love for her. He is driven almost mad, which I suppose excuses the lengths he goes to conquer her. And she, against her will, finds him handsome and compelling, making her virtue even more at risk. I do not need to remind you of Mr. Bennet's unkempt whiskers or that he is almost thirty or of his recent scratching himself in a most unseemly manner, I suspect the result of an infection by way of one of those mangy cats that scamper about the dairy. Still, I find the trials and tribulations of Pamela instructive. For instance, at the end of the scene, when Pamela's lord is a-quiver and she sees the Light, she faints.

Which is what I shall do when next my husband seeks to exercise his rights. I do not believe there can be such a thing as rights when all the rights belong to one person and none to the other. This teetering to one side is the cause of what we women are accused of: underhandedness. Sneakery is one way of living in the shadow of one's tyrant, and it is my way whenever I can think of something quickly enough because at every turn Mr. Bennet assures me that my rights extend only to the household staff and the children; the rest are his. "Do I not have rights pertaining to my own person?" I enquire. "You can wash when it suits you," he replies, "and you can choose your raiment." Pfah!

Shame and envy descend upon me when I think of Pamela, who has never ever pretended or prevaricated, who has been forthright in her protection of her virtue, of her very self. She wants only to be left alone, to be free from threat. On the other hand, Pamela does not have to devise a way to get her Master to a ball. I do. Because Mr. Bennet will surely not agree to attend, and if he does not, then neither can I. And I shall attend, no matter what I have to do to get there.

Now I must fly, for Mrs. Salther insists on punctuality

and of all people it is she I most fear to offend. Today I must ask her if she can make the bodice just a little looser, not loose, just not quite so binding. Pray for me, dear sister, and think me not the vain creature I fear I am.

First, though, I will just skip down to see what Cook has on the fire. I hope it is rice pudding, for if it is I shall spoon some into a bowl and plop a bit of marmalade on top. Pishtosh if Cook should carry on. I have my rights, after all.

Yr lvng sister

O Jane! I hasten to add to this letter before it is posted to you. Just as I was enjoying Cook's delicious pudding, who should come roaring into the house but Mr. Bennet, singing at the top of his lungs some tune I did not recognize with words I could not make out. He commanded me to come up from my eating and present myself upstairs. I could not do otherwise and so protested in my sweetest voice, my pudding-sweet voice.

Upstairs the door to my bedchamber had been flung open and Mr. Bennet stood within, grinning, his breeches down around his ankles. Such a sight no longer shocked me; indeed, it was almost laughable, but I managed to present myself as the demure young wife. And I pretended not to be appalled when he belted out, "Here comes the sun!" and danced about clicking his heels in the most ridiculous fashion. He held out his hand. Which I refused, prettily of course.

Having no idea what he was singing about or why, I argued that Mrs. Salther would be most put out with me if I were late to my fitting and begged his indulgence, fluttering my lashes, twirling deliciously so as to allow my curls to escape the cap, all in a most alluring fashion, or so I thought. "It will surely be a most beautiful gown," I said. "You will be proud to see me in it at the ball, which is but a few weeks away so ordering a coach and four at this time would not be too early, just as I have already ordered new gloves for you to go with the most elaborate new waistcoat, why, the embroidery itself will place you among the most distinguished of guests—"

He advanced on me, all a-glower now, tugging up his breeches so as to run after me should I try to escape. Oh my, I may have misfigured. "But, Mr. Bennet," I protested. "The servants—"

"Hang the servants," he bellowed. "Stop your prating, woman!" And he pressed me into the bed, where fortunately time did not stand still and he had his way with me. Briefly, I envied Pamela, who had escaped such violation, though as always thought of any kind was obliterated until he was finished with me. Afterward, we lay together, he spent, I cringing, in the muss of bedclothes when of a sudden a strange and unusual occurrence befell us. As I lay quietly weeping, he reached for me and pulled me to him. I have seen him do the very same with one of those wretched cats; he will scoop it up, clasp it to him, and smooth its coat until it is calm. And so he did with me.

I have never thought myself a wild cat or a wild woman, but I must admit to something in me that his stroking quieted. I felt an unfamiliar pleasure and then surprise for it was a sensation I thought never to have with this man who was my sworn enemy. As he held me he sang into my ear the words to the tune he had been shouting only minutes before, something about the sun. Nestled into that hollow where his shoulder seemed to promise warmth and comfort, I could make only a certain sense of his whispering, but I divined enough to return me to my senses, and I sat bolt upright. Here comes the son, indeed. We shall see about that.

I will be late to the fitting. Pray she will not turn me out.

Yrs in haste,

Ch. 10

In Which the Cursed Ball Refuses to Die

Quippe ubi fas versum atque nefas.

"Where wrong is right, and right wrong."

—VIRGIL

It was the coldest spring I can remember. I shivered as I tramped on the still-frozen paths that edged my fields. It was almost as cold outside as it was in. Mrs. Bennet was once more tight-lipped save for occasional rants directed at the servants. More than one of them have come to me and pleaded with me to intercede, or at least to try to make some sense of her raves. "I'll do what I can," I have promised, "but keep in mind that the work of running this house is the provenance of Mrs. Bennet, not mine, and her word is your command." I am sympathetic to my servants' complaints. Still, best not to contravene tradition and besides, I knew I could do nothing to stop her.

It is my opinion that she has no one to blame but herself for the chaos that thrives in my household. Mrs. Bennet has let the servants run willy-nilly, has never had a firm hand with them. She has let them ride roughshod over her orders and now she is reaping the "rewards." Take Mrs. Rummidge: She has been in my employ since the beginning of my marriage and in my view has lied up a storm, offering Mrs. Bennet advice that was always wrong and possibly harmful. To ingratiate herself with Mrs. Bennet and secure the position of—what exactly, I do not know—she had presented herself as a married woman with children when I knew from village talk that she was a spinster who had been dismissed from her job spinning, who had never been near a woman in labour let alone assist in childbirth, who claimed expertise in the prevention of pregnancy as well as the enhancement of it, whose experience with children was nil. She was an all-around liar and, I have no doubt, a thief. Yet it is this same Mrs. Rummidge who can quiet Elizabeth. It is Mrs. Rummidge my wife called for in the midst of her lying-in periods. It is a great mystery to me who all my life has relied on the truthfulness of fact.

Which was why, one day as I was idly toying with the little bottles and jars on Mrs. Bennet's dressing table, I came upon a bottle filled with something that looked and smelled like vinegar.

"What is this?" I asked my wife, holding up the bottle.

She looked away. This was one of her silent periods. "What, pray tell?" Silence. "Must I use force?" I persisted.

Speech was once more hers. "You would use force, wouldn't you. You would strike me. You are as brutish as any man I have ever known. And furthermore, I will scream even if you don't strike me and the servants will come running and then they will run through the village crying how you bully and beat your poor wife, the mother of your children and so recently, too." She made ready to scream.

"Cease your nonsense," I said. "You are a silly goose. You know I would never do you bodily harm, you know that. But you drive me to extremes, you do. And if I may address another of your threats, the servants." Mrs. Bennet put her hands over her ears. "You know very well that, should you scream, the servants would stay right where they are. You know they are too lazy to run anywhere, least of all into the village. And if they did run into the village, no one there would believe them. They are the dregs of the serving class; no one in the village would hire them and so they are here, where they show every evidence of remaining. To our eternal regret."

"Vinegar," said Mrs. Bennet. "It's vinegar in the bottle." She sat on the edge of her bed, her toes not quite touching the floor, kicking the air.

"Vinegar! How on earth did vinegar come to sit on your dressing table?"

"That's all I will say. You asked what the bottle held and I answered. It's vinegar. Now if you will leave me, sir. My head is splitting. I would lie down . . . if it please my lord."

"You needn't mock," I answered. "It ill becomes you."

"Tell Cook we will dine at four." She lay back onto the bed, eyes closed against me and all the unpleasantness she thought me to represent. Misbegotten charges, all of them.

"Until four, then." On the way down to the kitchen I realized that the mystery had only deepened. Vinegar but for what? Was she ill? Was this vinegar a medicine of some kind? I began to worry and was surprised that I was.

I have never liked surprises, and mysteries are full of them. My wife was full of both. It had never occurred to me when I saw her gay little face and pretty little figure two years ago that I might do well to investigate her manner and enquire into her thoughts. Instead, I had assumed, thereby making an ass of myself, that this girl would be a younger version of my mother, now dead these seven years. My mother had been like me, calm and composed, steady and reliable. She had kept a fine table and she had kept the servants within the bounds of their duties. I had never known her to give herself over to moodiness, nor had I ever heard her complain or throw herself onto the bed in a pout. Order had prevailed. She was, in my beloved Milton's words, a "bright-harnest Angel who sits in order serviceable." And now this. Had my mother lived, none of this current disorderliness would last the day. But she was not alive and this girl I had married was, and the mess she had created promised to continue unabated.

I trudged out to Tom's field to see how Tom and his new drill were getting on with the planting of the turnips. It would calm me to watch someone go about his duties so methodically and so unquestioningly. Besides, I will admit to the need to confide in someone—clearly that someone was not my wife—for I had received a letter on that very day. It announced the visit of my cousin and heir to Longbourn, that is if Mrs. Bennet fails to live up to her responsibility to bear a son. Francis Collins was coming to call. Mrs. Bennet would have comport herself in a manner so far barely in evidence.

"Weather's no good for planting, sir," said Tom. "No telling if the drill will do the trick, the ground's still frozen." And just as I was about to confide, or at least explain my anxiety over Collins's visit, Tom said, "We'd best hope for some sun to warm the earth. Good day to you, sir." And he left me to stand in the cold of an April spring hoping for some sun to warm my world.

In the house I found Mrs. Bennet newly risen from her bed of pain and seated now in the parlour close to the fire, where she busied herself with her eternal embroidery. I have yet to see a finished piece or where it went when finished, perhaps on undergarments I was restricted from beholding. "We must have a conversation," I said. "Terribly cold this spring." Outside the rain slashed at the windows. At least, I thought, it isn't hail; things could be worse.

"About what?" She looked at me balefully. "Not the weather surely."

"About this ball you would have me attend."

Mrs. Bennet brightened. "I will happily converse with you about the ball. Let us begin by your agreeing that you will accompany me without protest."

"I will," I said.

"You will?" She secured her needle in the cloth and set the hoop aside. She looked at me and smiled.

Months had passed since I had seen a smile from her, or from anyone in this melancholy household. I was encouraged. "Yes," I answered.

"And how are we to get there?" Her suspicions were renewed. "Shall we go by dogcart? Will we walk? Shall we ask someone in the village to haul us in their wheelbarrow?"

There seemed to be no end to her creativity. I answered quickly, "Of course not. We will arrive at this ball in a proper carriage drawn by a proper horse."

The corners of her mouth turned down. "One? One horse?"

"All right, two."

"Oh, my dear husband!" She leapt from her chair and made toward me as if to throw her arms about my neck but pulled up just short. Suspicion had not yet left the room.

"By what intervention have you come to your senses? Why such a change? What are you up to?" She sat back down and pulled her chair nearer the fire.

Reeling from the possibility of a wifely embrace—it would have been her first, mine, too—I blurted, "My cousin is coming to visit." The storm outside, which had abated during the conversation, started afresh. This time it looked as if the rain would turn to hail. The branches slashed at the windows, and I moved closer to the fire. Mrs. Bennet did also and there we sat almost touching, certainly within reach of each other. We stared into the fire.

"Your cousin Collins?" she asked. "The cousin who might someday inherit Longbourn? The cousin who could very well put me and my children out into the storm?"

"That one," I said. It seemed to have gotten colder. I tossed another bundle onto the fire. "He will arrive Friday next."

"Why?" She threw down her embroidery and began to stride up and down the room, her skirts switching noisily against the floor.

"His letter claims he will be passing through and longs to see his only living cousin."

Mrs. Bennet paused in her tramping and said, "Bosh! He is coming to put his hands on what is mine, ours, yours."

"I believe you are right, my dear. What do you suggest we do?"

"Short of garroting, drawing and quartering, poisoning, lambasting him with your walking stick, and drowning him in a butt of malmsey, I don't think there is much we can do." She stood stock-still, amazed at herself. I stared at her in wonderment. Wherever did she find those words? Had she been reading? I could think of only one writer who might supply such variety—Shakespeare. Had she been at my library? Would her surprises never end?

"I could write and tell him you are ill," I said, "that we are all ill—"

"—That the plague has come to our house, that the pox has infected us all, that our streams and fields are rife with disease. . . . No," she said, "he would never believe our lie." She was quiet. She returned to the chair near the fire and, looking directly into my eyes, said, "I think our only choice is to behave with all the dignity within us and impress him with the certitude that all is well and that he will have to live to be a hundred in order to inherit something that is not rightfully his."

I smiled.

"We'll leave the last part out," she said and smiled, too.

"Indeed," I said. "We shall simply keep calm and carry on."

"So then," said Mrs. Bennet, "a carriage and two?"

Ch. 11

Dear Sister,

Please forgive the brevity of this note. I write primarily to tell you that I think of you and pray for Mr. Phillips's improved health every hour of the day. The current weather cannot be conducive to his recovery. Can you recall a colder spring?

I remember his laboured breaths during your last visit. You are, I know, the best remedy for anything that ails him. Your patience and calmness are themselves healers and your affection for your husband is itself balm. I look forward to a visit when the roads can be made passable. Just now they are icy ruts and our light carriage would make travel an arduous and even dangerous affair. In the meantime, you are much in my thoughts.

Good fortune continues to provide us with good health here at Longbourn. Mr. Bennet was for a time afflicted with an unexplained irritation to the skin which caused much irascibility in his person, albeit freedom from assault for me. It seems to have abated and except for a recent verbal outburst against what he calls my poor administration of the household he has returned to his usual glum distractability. To you and to you only I will confide that in some ways he is right: the servants do whatever pleases them, often nothing; and I must confess, though again only to you, that I do not quite know what orders to give or how to give them. "Stop lazing about," does not seem to stop their lazing about. "You said something, ma'am?" they respond, often without the "ma'am," and then resume what I am to think is an industrious task. Our mother's tea service shows no evidence of such labour, so what they are polishing is forever a mystery. I do not know what to do but do something I must.

I would never blame our dear mother for my shortcomings but I do wish she had taught us something about servants (though we had only two). Granted, she did teach us to set a fine table. Thank heavens for that. And here at Longbourn, from happenstance, we have a wonderful cook who does as she pleases, which in turn pleases all who partake of her talents. As for the rest, they do as little as possible, which is very little indeed. The linens are thrown into the laundry, where they remain until Mr. Bennet orders that his bedsheets be renewed. In the evening, as he stands next to the fire, he runs his finger along the mantel, marking a path through the dust that has accumulated thereon, then holds his dusty finger up to me. I busy myself with my embroidery. Sweeping? The dust on the floors rivals the dust elsewhere. And the children? What of the children? Oh dear, I am going on much longer than I had planned or than you have time to read, but . . .

Mrs. Rummidge, of whom you may have heard me speak, sees to both Jane and Elizabeth so I do not fear for their well-being though Mr. B. would not agree with me here, either. But the children are washed and fed—neither is at my breast any longer—and despite their differences in character do seem to get along. They are in the nursery most of their waking hours or, when weather permits, bouncing along a path in their perambulator, Mrs. Rummidge pushing them along. Lately, however, both the girls have begun to behave in ways that concern both Mr. B. and me. There is much pushing and shoving and even striking. The other day, as they sat on the flagstone path, Elizabeth reached for Jane's nose and pulled hard. Jane shrieked and struck her sister in her little tummy and both tumbled about the ground, where they rolled and pummeled each other as if they were two little boys! Mrs. Rummidge scooped them up and all three came back to the house out of sorts and sulky. I must admit that this sort of behaviour may be the result of the arguing they see and hear between their mother and their father, though of course we have never struck each other in ways visible to the naked eye. But I must confess that we are all here embattled in some unknowable way against I know not what, perhaps the general untidiness of our household or more I cannot ascertain. When we are not quarreling in the common rooms, Mr. Bennet resides in his library, I in my bedchamber. One of us—or both—will have to emerge. I suspect that it will be I.

And now amidst all this disarray and my own preparations for the ball only weeks away I am told that we are to be visited by Mr. Bennet's cousin, Mr. Collins. It is a visit to be dreaded by all concerned except for young Mr. Collins, who surely intends to lay hands on what he presumes will one day be his. We shall see about that.

Have you secured your own copy of *Pamela*? If so, then you have also secured a hiding place for it. Secrets are delicious, are they not.

Affectionately,
MB

Ch. 12

In Which a Visitor Appears

Equidem plura transcribo quam credo.

"Truly, I set down more things than I believe."

—QUINTUS CURTIUS

The present cannot be depended upon to predict the future. I would come to know my cousin in later years after he had turned into a wrinkly fuss-budget with a lisp and a leer. When he came to us, on his first visit to Longbourn, his hair had not yet receded. His midsection had not been force-fed into prominence. His eyes were free of the spectacles that would identify him (wrongly) as a serious man with religious convictions. He betrayed not even a hint of the toady he would become. Then, at eighteen, Mr. Collins was what one might call, if one was seventeen and female, a looker: tall, slim, with a ruddy complexion and broad shoulders.

I did indeed stop short at the sight of this hale and hearty young cousin who might someday own and live in and rule the remains of myself and my property. Intolerable. In the meantime, I would continue to do my duty as the progenitor of heirs, thus staving off any presumption by this upstart cousin that might despoil the tranquil future I envisioned for myself and my multitudinous family, among whom there would be a boy. This Collins fellow looked to be a threat. He looked as if he might any minute drive a cart into the drawing room and tack up a sign over the hearth announcing "It's Mine." I began to enact the role that I and Mrs. Bennet had created for me.

"Mr. Bennet!" my wife cried. "Take heed of the mud you have brought with you onto our carpet! Must I remind you always?"

"Good news, old girl," I shouted. "We have some mud at last. The ground seems to be softening somewhat; at least, the ice is melting and so we have this! Good, clean mud!" As if noticing Mr. Collins for the first time, I strode toward him, tracking mud across the Aubusson as I did, and held out my hand be-gloved and grimy. "Halloa, young cousin! I remember you as but a lad." I looked him up and down. "You have changed, my boy, and for the better, I'd say. You were a sorry runt, if memory serves. How goes the health of your parents?" I tore off my gloves. "Please excuse me; these gloves have come to be a part of me, so often do I find them necessary in my dawn-to-dusk labours. I sometimes forget I once used to be a gentleman." I sighed loudly. "No longer. I am a farmer, no more nor less than my tenant Tom, who of course steals from me at every turn and must be scolded and threatened almost daily."

Old girl? Mrs. Bennet seemed to take umbrage, as if to say that already I was over-acting. "Now, husband," she said, "leave off your tales of woe. Our young cousin has come to make himself acquainted with the delights of Longbourn."

I grumbled something about there being no delights and plumped myself down on the settee next to Mr. Collins, who sat stroking its velvet cover. "So, young sir," I said, clapping him upon the knee, "what say you to picking up a spade on the morrow to see if the earth has warmed enough for us farmers to begin to work it?"

So fine a performance was I giving that Mrs. Bennet almost believed it. In truth, I had rarely lifted a spade or any other tool during the whole of my life at Longbourn. I had borrowed Tom's field gloves that were indeed scarred and worn with hard work, and I had kicked away the ice on the path in order to muddy my boots. Most unusual of all was my manner. My wife had never seen me in what she called a jovial mood; she had rarely seen me even cheerful. And she had never ever seen me welcome someone to Longbourn with such heartfelt sincerity as I displayed now. Even her own sister's visit had not elicited the warmth she saw now bestowed upon the young man who would steal her rightful home from under her and her children.

Hildy, the new parlour maid, appeared from the vestibule. "Mr. and Mrs. Littleworth have arrived," she said, dimpling in Mr. Collins's direction and reddening when he grinned boldly at her. That girl will have to go, I thought. I looked anew at this cousin and marveled at the animal vigour he possessed, which I had never had, and now, the prisoner of middle age, never would. Alas.

Mr. and Mrs. Littleworth, who lived not far from Longbourn, were the wealthiest, the oldest, and the fattest couple in the county. They were also the dullest, or so I thought then. They had been invited so that they, too, could act out their parts, in this case being themselves. They would surely bore young Collins back to Buddington. I and Collins rose from the settee.

"We came by cart," bellowed Mr. Littleworth as best he could. "Don't remember all those steps out front. Not so easy to make it up the lot of them," he gasped.

"And did you notice," said Mrs. Bennet, "that they're crumbling?" She glanced meaningfully at Collins, who was moving in the direction of Hildy.

"We came by cart, indeed we did," said Mrs. Littleworth, bending her right ear in the direction of her husband's voice. From this somewhat peculiar angle, she explained, "Mr. Littleworth wishes to save the carriage for more formal excursions; he prides himself on his thrift and insists that he can drive the cart without benefit of a coachman or a footman or any person who might make our journey comfortable. Isn't that right, my dear?" she shouted. "And wouldn't you say that your cart jolted us near to breaking our bones!"

"Yes, jolted us, keeps costs down," Mr. Littleworth answered.

"Such a spring we're having!" Mrs. Littleworth leaned into her husband, exposing the enormity of one breast, and added, "But it will no doubt be our last." She poked him in the general area of his ribs with her elbow and winked, this time at Mrs. Bennet. "You're a pretty little thing," she said.

"Most likely our last, yes," Mr. Littleworth said; then he pulled himself upright and pronounced, "One certainty remains, however; we have not lost our appetites." Clearly, Mr. Littleworth's appetite had followed him all the days of his life, for his belly tormented the seams of his waistcoat, from which the buttons dangled uselessly. Mrs. Littleworth giggled and elbowed him again in the ribs. "Don't do that, my dear," he said. She poked him again and cackled. Mr. Littleworth raised his hand.

Quickly Mrs. Bennet motioned toward Collins. "This is our cousin, Mr. Collins, visiting our county for a bit. It is his first visit, you see." Mr. Collins held out his hand.

"It's not getting any lighter out there," said Mr. Littleworth, ignoring the hand and pointing his sausage-sized finger at the window. "Don't like to eat by candlelight and then, well, we'll have to gird our loins for the ride home."

"Girding our loins," Mrs. Littleworth chortled. "Could be our last." She made as if to elbow him again, but her husband held her off with, "How soon can we expect dinner?"

Hildy, having been the object of handsome young Collins's attention ever since his arrival, stood scarlet-faced and breathing heavily at the door to the dining room. "Dinner is served," she said and rolled her eyes. With young Collins so attentive, serving such a dinner as her mistress had commanded made for much humiliation. This dinner made no sense to her, nor did it to Cook in the kitchen below, whose tears of shame salted the chicken livers. Such a dinner would please no one, nor would it satisfy anyone's appetite.

Mr. Littleworth tucked his napkin under his chin and looked hopeful. Mrs. Littleworth, from across the table, heaved her bosom upward to prevent it from interfering with her lap and winked at no one in particular. Mr. Collins took his seat on Mrs. Bennet's right, in direct view of Hildy, and rubbed his hands together. He raised his empty wine glass and said, "Here's to a fine repast and to the friends and family who will share it. Exceedingly lovely crystal, good cousin. Ravenscroft, is it not?" I nodded and noted silently that already he was taking stock of what his future might hold, young buzzard that he is.

"You may serve now," said Mrs. Bennet to Hildy, who, eyes lowered and lips trembling, did. She required almost no time to place it all on the table: soup, a joint, a pudding, pickles, jellies, and a fowl. Mr. Littleworth looked doubtful.

"I do hope the turtle kept well in the cooling shed," said Mrs. Bennet as she ladled soup from the tureen into bowls. She nodded to Hildy and said, "Bring our guests some ale. Or claret if they would prefer." She explained to her guests, "This weather has prevented our chapman from delivering to us the meats of the sea; where once we would be partaking of a salmon and perhaps a turbot, we shall have to settle for pork and potatoes from our very own farm. And of course a guinea hen." She sighed. So did the Littleworths. Ale and claret? Poor substitutes for the sherry and hock they had anticipated, not to mention the absence of an entire course. Surely someone could have found a fish somewhere.

I hacked at the shoulder of pork, cursing the absence of veal. "My apologies, we simply could not keep the pork as fresh as we had hoped. I trust this will be to your liking even so. The sauce is ample for spreading, a good cover for whatever lies beneath, ha-ha. And we can look forward to nuts and raisins, again from our very own Longbourn." I cast a benevolent smile down the table. My new role was turning out to be great fun!

The Littleworths appeared downcast. A wretched cart ride and now this scrap dinner with libations fit for the servants. Mr. Littleworth tried for conversation. "I hear your man Tom is selling his wife's weaving in the village. Doing quite well, I understand." Nods all 'round. "Careful there, Edward, he might buy his farm right out from under you."

Mr. Collins, who gave new meaning to the word "exuberance," said, "Oh, I do believe that e'en so Longbourn will remain the substantial holding it is. And so beautiful." He gave himself back over to smiling in the direction of Hildy.

Mrs. Littleworth took her turn: "And the Dalrymple girl is with child, no father in sight. Tsk. Tsk. And of course our new neighbour, Colonel Millar, I believe he is called. A most handsome fellow, I understand, and surely in command of quite a fortune, given his purchase of Northfield."

Mrs. Bennet, at the end of the table, stopped her fork in midair. Without pausing to empty her mouth of her previous biteful, she said, "Yes, he has taken that grand house very near to us. We look forward to making his acquaintance. Do you know," she asked, bits of guinea hen churning in her mouth, "if he brings with him a Mrs. Millar?" She turned to Hildy. "Serve the burgundy."

"I seem to recall mention of a Mrs. Somebody, a Mrs. Jewkes, something like that," said Mrs. Littleworth, who had long since finished her small portions of a small meal and sat slumped in her chair, picking at bits of fowl hiding in her lap. Not finding enough to bother with and mostly small bones, she tossed back the last of her single serving of claret, Mrs. Bennet seeming to have corralled the burgundy. "They are said to be inseparable, she and the colonel."

Mrs. Bennet sat rigid in her chair, her cheeks pale, her eyes fixed on a distant point. "A housekeeper, perhaps," she said, and drained her glass.

"And he brings with him a younger woman also, I believe," said Mrs. Littleworth.

"A veritable harem," said Mr. Littleworth, rousing himself from a close-on slumber, his napkin lonely and virginal on the floor beneath.

"His sister, no doubt," said Mrs. Bennet, slurring a bit on "sister."

I looked at her sharply and interrupted. "This Millar fellow is the cause of a serious worry." I turned to Collins, who was partaking liberally of the sack that had appeared only moments before from the mysteries of Hildy's apron. "He has made claim to the westernmost plot of Longbourn, insisting that without fencing one cannot be sure of where Longbourn ends and his estate begins." Collins was busying himself with sipping. I continued, this time more loudly. "My hope is that I can in the most neighbourly fashion convince him that enclosure, whilst the coming practice in the north counties, is not now nor has ever been the rule in our county. We have no need for fences; gentlemen's agreements are all that are necessary. 'Just look about you,' I will say to him. He will see that custom and tradition take precedence over the here and now." No one appeared to be listening to me, not even out of politeness. Collins poured himself another glass of sack, and I hurried to make my point, this time at full volume. "If this Millar fellow has his way, what you see now of Longbourn is not necessarily what you will see of it in the future." Collins set aside the empty decanter and resumed ogling Hildy. In a final push I shouted, "It could be very small. One man could, simply by way of fencing, claim ownership of land not his." At this I stood up from my chair at the foot of the table and said with all the force at my command, "One man could reign over an entire county!"

At that very moment the tray laden with the bone china left me by my mother slipped from Hildy's hands. The crash resounded throughout the house. It couldn't have helped but wake the children upstairs and roused the servants below. Mrs. Littleworth blinked rapidly with both eyes. Her husband slumbered on. I stood transfixed by the sight of my shattered past. Hildy shrieked and fled. Collins bent down to discover if any piece, any piece at all, might have escaped destruction. "So sad," he murmured. "Nothing left."

"Exactly!" I cried. "You get my point!" I sat down.

Mrs. Bennet sat rigid in her chair. After what seemed like a very long time she stood and, stepping carefully so as to avoid the shards of china and the pool of burgundy seeping into the carpet, said, "Shall we repair to the drawing room for port?"

"Ladies, too?" asked Mrs. Littleworth. Would there be nothing normal about this evening? "I do not smoke cigars," she said and made as if to poke her husband. He raised his hand halfway.

"Yes," said Mrs. Bennet. "Any port in a storm." She giggled and stumbled slightly as she led the way into the drawing room. I looked on in amazement. Collins regained his smile, though, like Mrs. Littleworth's blinking, it no longer seemed to have a target.

Evening's end couldn't come quickly enough for the Littleworths. "Come, my dear," said a suddenly solicitous Mrs. Littleworth. "We don't want you out after dark now, do we." Briskly she bundled both of them into greatcoats and hurried to the cart, not at all apprehensive over the jumbling and jolting they would surely suffer on their way home. Mrs. Littleworth, from her perch on the cart, waved farewell and called, "See you next at the ball. And you, dear child"—she pointed to Mrs. Bennet—"be your most beautiful. I shall send you the name of my seamstress."

Oh yes, the ball. I put my arm around Mrs. Bennet, who, unsteady on her feet, seemed to be listing to the right. "Get hold of yourself," I commanded. She leaned left. "Straighten up," I said. She continued to teeter.

Young Collins, for his part, appeared to have enjoyed the entire evening despite the ruination of a small portion of his inheritance. "Now to bed," he exclaimed. "Tomorrow promises to be long and arduous. I look forward to it. Good night, dear cousins."

In my bedroom I lay awake far into the night, as I can only assume my wife did in hers. How was it possible for anyone to get a night's rest with all that ruckus from young Collins's room? The laughter was not just his; a girl's, too, probably Hildy's, I reckoned. I tugged at myself briefly in the forlorn hope of joining the party if only from afar. From her room, I could hear Mrs. Bennet, her headache for the morrow already in full force, as she wept into her pillow.

The dark hours of the night did nothing to console her, and at last, unable to bear the sound of her weeping, I crept into her bedchamber. Seating myself on the edge of the bedstead, I patted her upon her shoulder and murmured, "There, there."

"There is nothing that is right," she sobbed. "Our cousin delights himself with what he sees as the bounty of our home, not at all what we had planned for." A fresh burst of tears beset her. "I disgraced you with my behaviour. I took on too much wine. I grew tipsy. I am so ashamed."

"There, there." I patted.

She sobbed anew. "You are my husband. You have a right to my obedience," she said. "I pray that I can repent of my rebellious spirit."

Things were going swimmingly right then. I moved my hand to my wife's back, which I stroked with all the gentleness at my command until her weeping subsided. She turned to me and laid her face upon my chest. I drew myself onto the bed. She did not push away my hand when I laid it gently on her breast. She did not flinch when I drew away her nightdress. She did not tense when I found my way below. Instead, she grew warm and efflorent, like the burgeoning springtime outside her very window, and then I do believe, that because of my efforts, she was lifted beyond anything she had known.

I could not have known it then, but in those moments of tenderness and joy, Edward, Jr., was conceived.

Ch. 13

The Cold of Late April

Dearest Jane,

This I swear: I shall never again allow wine or spirits to pass my lips. I shall abstain from that which might cause me to lose my good sense, my good manners, and my resolve to live as a self-respecting wife and mother of two. You may take this as an oath. Should you see me slip from it, I expect your reprimand and even a slight rap upon the knuckles. But I swear to live by my new principles. Come to think of it, I did not have much in the way of old principles. But now I have. And I do believe that the visit from our cousin, the young Mr. Collins, prompted the changes within me. Let me descry that visit as clearly as my memory will allow.

To begin at the beginning, I was taken by surprise by Mr. Collins's manly appearance. I had expected a person of many years, so imagine my surprise when this vibrant, strapping young fellow, appearing to be about the same age as I, stepped over the doorsill. He stood in the vestibule of Longbourn and beamed at me. "So this is Longbourn," he said. "And you must be its mistress." He bowed deeply. "Happy is the house lit by such loveliness."

Unaccustomed to alliteration, I steadied myself on the newel post and stammered a welcome, managed a slight nod of the head, and breathed a sigh of relief when Hildy, the purported downstairs maid, entered, curtsied, and held out her arms for Mr. Collins's greatcoat. Odd that until now Hildy's dimples had remained a secret. I frowned but briefly, then ushered Mr. Collins into the drawing room, where, I assured him, Mr. Bennet would join him shortly. "He is so terribly caught up in the misery of what would seem to be a disastrously shortened growing season," I said. "He spends all his daylight hours conferring with his tenants over planting and harvesting, with detecting signs of poachers and collecting carcasses of deer and grouse and . . ."

Mr. Collins seemed not to hear me so intent was he in staring at the carpet. "This is quite a fine Aubusson you have here," he said. "Should last a good long while."

"Good heavens no," I lied, "I could show you the worn spots were it not for the embarrassment they would cause me. Oh dear, I am prattling on. Forgive me."

This was the tack Mr. Bennet and I had settled on when news of Collins's visit reached us. We would make life at Longbourn look like hard work. We would point to the shabbiness of the furniture within; we would lament the hours spent outdoors in the unforgiving fields, the unkempt gardens, the wreckage of paths, the impassable roads, the declining forests, hopeful that in so doing Collins would leave off any interest in owning such a property and go away.

"Ah," said Mr. Collins, warming himself at the small fire in the grate. "I have spent much of my life in the out-of-doors and revel in hard work." He took a deep breath and let it out slowly. "Fine mantelpiece this. Good strong oak would be my guess." He smoothed his hand along its surface.

I allowed my glance to linger a bit on young Collins's upper self, which appeared to be rippling, and on his strong young hand so gentle on my mantelpiece. "Indeed," I murmured. "Indeed."

"I would be delighted to give a hand to my dear cousin. And of course"—he bowed ever so gallantly—"to you, dear lady."

I moved away from the fire, whose warmth had spread to my cheeks. "And of course," I stammered, "there are the property disputes." I had no idea whatsoever what property disputes were, only that Mr. Bennet had told me to mention them last, insisting that they would provide good and final reason for a would-be owner to reconsider before he made a final decision. So far as I knew, which was not very far at all, there were no property disputes, at least not at Longbourn.

Surely you can see, dear sister, how deceitful I have become, how easily I told untruths, how deliberately I arranged for our cousin to draw false conclusions, how, even, I may have flirted a bit with the young man. But that is not all. And that is not the worst.

You have for some years now thought me flighty and even selfish, although your love and patience never flagged. I have come to see the truth of your judgements. For here—and once again I beg your indulgence—I come to confess that in a moment of inebriation I allowed Mr. Bennet to seduce me. Ah! I cannot bear to write the word! I cannot bear to recall that night; in fact, I can*not* recall that night, so hugely had I indulged in wines of all sorts. I know only that when I woke I screamed, for a stranger lay beside me, his face hidden in the pillows so that I could not at first recognize that it was indeed Mr. Bennet, my husband and the man whose embraces I had shunned for the past two years. At my scream he picked his face up from the pillow and grinned. Grinned! "Good morning, my dear," he said as if his spending the night in my bed was a natural occurrence. Needless to say I screamed again and he bolted. Let us hope that Mrs. Rummidge's vinegar douche prevented any mishap.

Dear sister, I am so ashamed. Whatever transpired during that horrible night lies buried in my memory, where it will remain forever. I write this now to expunge the fact of it and to promise to regain my virtue by whatsoever means I can discover. Despite all that has happened, I remain faithful to my one true love, my colonel with whom I shall be reunited in only a few short weeks. I am no less a virgin now than when we first met.

It is good that the time for the ball draws near. Preparations are enormous; my dress alone requires the constant attention and talents of seamstresses. Its cost, at first a source of uneasiness for me, so extravagant did even I consider it, is now no more than I earned last night. I am due more than Mr. Bennet can ever repay. I have earned the right to be as extravagant as I wish. I have earned the right to pursue my own happiness without the slightest concern for the well-being of my husband. I have earned the right to protect and defend the futures of my children, to see to it that my daughters marry well and grow strong. I would that I could be a more dutiful wife, but such is not within my power today.

Please be kind.

Yrs truly,
Marianne

P.S. As mistress of this house I have decided to take the servants in hand. They have become disrespectful and unruly. Alas, where to begin? I suppose by learning their names. Only Hildy for some reason stands out.

Ch. 14

In Which Melancholy Pays a Visit

His se stimulis dolor ipse lacessit.

"With these incitements grief provokes itself."

—LUCRETIUS

John Milton's "Doctrine and Discipline of Divorce" spoke to me at this particular moment in a way that the poet's sonnet on youth and time had spoken in years past. I was no longer young. I had recently turned thirty and found myself not as spry as I had been only a few years earlier when I danced my way into marital misery, our recent and most pleasant coupling notwithstanding. All the proof of aging I needed was the memory of trying to keep up with my young cousin as together we dug at making a furrow. Collins, forever exuberant, handled his spade as if he had been born to it. My back began to hurt with the first turn of earth and to worsen into the third day. My future looked bleak, filled with melancholy most serious and chronic. I was, in Milton's words, "a sad spirit wedded to loneliness."

"The preservation of life is more worth than the compulsory keeping of marriage." Milton's words leapt from the page. I slumped lower in the chair, hoping to ease the pain in my back and to hide myself from servants and from the children and Mrs. Bennet. No one was allowed into my library unless invited and so far no one had been invited, certainly not young Collins for whom this library might promise the comfort and contentment I had found for myself for lo these many years. In truth, I had never been as young as Collins. I had never been full to bursting with Collins's animal spirits. I had never looked into the future with optimism, with hope, with enthusiasm. I had been a plodder, not much of this, less of that. It was only here in this library that I found communion and solace and escape from the person I feared myself to be.

Mrs. Bennet has resumed her silence, although this current muteness differs from previous periods in that this one is accompanied by baleful stares and swift retreats whenever I chance to come upon her. She scurries about the house, quick to leave a room in which I am occupied, quicker still to absent herself from a room I enter. She nibbles at her dinner and excuses herself almost as soon as I enter the dining room. She is like a mouse, quiet, swift, and merciless. In the evening she repairs to her bedchamber and emerges in midmorning when I am sure to be seeing to the estate in the fields beyond.

"When a man is confronted by the sight of his deluded thoughts . . ." wrote Milton. I had deluded myself into believing that marriage, that my marriage in particular, would prove a cure for my loneliness. Yes, I needed an heir and only a wife could give me one. So far she had failed me in this. But I had from an early age known myself to be of a depressive nature, and I had hoped that this delightful slip of a girl would provide surcease from the weight of my thoughts and the solitary life I had led so far. Here, too, she had failed me.

As had Milton. "They also serve who only stand and wait." In my younger years, that line had served me well, but as I aged, I found myself deluded once again, for I had stood and I had waited, but doing so had not resulted in a service to anyone; in fact, my very presence appeared to be, certainly in the eyes of my wife, a disservice.

From the kitchen rooms below, I can hear the sound of her voice in some sort of remonstrance. Clearly she has no difficulty expressing herself to others, in this instance the servants. "I am mistress here!" I hear. At last. Only good can come from that. Loud noises of discontent. And from someone, "A bit late, ain't you."

I return John Milton, stiff in black leather, to my bookcase. Outside the window, spring has sprung. The woodbine flowers along the trellis, the primrose edges the paths, the larches have turned from black to green, the songs of birds are everywhere, and soon the wisteria vine will burst with blossoms. I can hear the rippling of the streams. Ice is gone. Rebirth is everywhere. Except in my own house.

A great sorrow overcame me. Only a few nights previously I had held my wife in my arms. She had been warm and soft and responsive. She returned my caresses and welcomed mine. She hid her face in the crook of my neck and murmured of her love for me and for our daughters. I am filled with shame to admit here on this page that I, Mr. Edward Bennet, had never before made love, nor had love been made to me. I scarcely knew what to do until the sighs and murmurs of my wife as she guided my hands over her breasts and beneath her gown brought me to my natural self and all else followed and was right. We slept entwined until the early hours of the morning when suddenly, just after daybreak, she opened her eyes and screamed. What was that about? I sighed then as I do now because I will never know. Immediately, she exchanged her screams for silence, and now despite the budding of the natural world outside the window, inside is cold and sere. In only seconds she returned me to the loneliness that had been mine before her presence brought me hope. Now hope seems dashed forever.

From below stairs I hear, "My house, my rules. You will do as I say or be replaced by those who will. Is that understood?" Silence.

Take heart, dear reader. All is not lost. For, oblivious to the tribulations of her parents, little Elizabeth, on leave from her wet nurse's cottage, has scooted into the library. At that age, Jane crawled about on hands and knees. Elizabeth does not crawl. She sits firmly upright and, tiny hands planted on the floor, little heels digging into the carpet, she scutters about the house on her small bottom wherever she pleases. Indeed, I almost tripped over her as I turned away from the window. "Oh now, look who's here!" I exclaimed and swept her up into my arms. Elizabeth gurgled in delight as I, her father, lifted her high up and then down and then up and then down. "Let us have a sit-down, shall we, Elizabeth," I said and settled us both into my reading chair. Elizabeth curled herself contentedly into my lap and laid her head on my chest. She smelled like the fresh air of spring and her cheeks were pink like the primroses just outside. Her skin was petal-smooth and her tiny body pliant and trusting. I held her tight and murmured into her mop of red curls: "When I consider how my light is spent, / Ere half my days in this dark world and wide . . ." Elizabeth's eyelids drooped and so did mine. Thus did Mrs. Bennet discover us. Anyone looking on would have sworn that the corners of her mouth turned up.

Ch. 15

May at Longbourn

Dearest Jane,

It was to be my finest hour. As you know, I had looked forward to Colonel Millar's ball for months, and recent events—the announcement that he had arrived at Northfield with an unknown woman—made my attendance at that ball fraught with peril beyond even my imagination. I would need to look my best no matter the cost to my husband.

As you know, my gown was made from the finest silk, fawn in colour, shot through with silver. I would shimmer as I glided about the floor. The bodice—a work of art if I do say so myself—woven of threads of silver and silk and gold, engirdled my waist, ending in a point to accent my slimness. No one could know that I had given birth to two. The neckline was cut low, just low enough to suggest the fullness of breasts beneath, but no lower. Because my gown's sleeves were relatively short, I wore long gloves the colour of ivory, which reached to my elbows, leaving a small portion of my upper arms bare and, if I do say so myself, enticingly plump. My pannier filled out the skirt of the gown so that room would have to be made for me as I arrived in the chaise and two that I inveigled Mr. Bennet to procure for this signal event. My dress would announce me to everyone as I came through the entrance and up the stairs, as I floated up to my colonel, so handsome, awaiting me in the receiving line.

Now I know, dear sister, that there are those who would accuse me of fostering a silly illusion. Those same persons—perhaps you—would argue that two years had passed since our first and only meeting, and that he and I had led full and different lives e'er since. But I would answer that surely his taking a house adjacent to my garden, not far from my favourite walking path, signified an awareness on his part of my presence, and if my conjectures were false, then that fate was taking a role in my future. Not having thought very much, if at all, about fate—what is it anyway?—I preferred to believe that the colonel sought me out and intended this ball to re-introduce himself to me in a polite and gentlemanly manner. If the ball—and my future—was in the hands of fate, then let fate be kind. Thusly, I prayed.

It should not surprise you that I chose not to wear jewels of any kind, nor would it surprise you that Mr. Bennet appeared relieved when I announced this decision. Instead, I wore an ivory-hued velvet riband around my neck. It begged to be touched. As did I.

Now indulge me, dear sister. Bear with me while I try to remember and relive those wondrous moments before my world came crashing down. Our carriage and two brought us to the steps of Northfield just a bit after eight. Northfield is a magnificent house, more like a palace than a country house, three entrances along the front, wings on either side. Grand, very grand. I had never visited here, not ever. Mr. Bennet, in an aside, mentioned that he had come here often as a boy. Why did I not know that? How is it that he could not bring himself to tell me? I could have teased him into presenting me here before this time. Perhaps then I might have become something more than a country wife and perpetual mother. Bear with me, Jane, while I take a new breath.

Now, then. We arrived at the middle entrance and were conducted to the entrance hall where a staircase ascended to the upper gallery. The floors were marble and our footsteps echoed; it was as if we were in a cathedral. Upstairs we made our way into the receiving line. Just ahead of us the Littleworths waited their turn. Mrs. Littleworth nodded approvingly at me, at my gown, for indeed it had been she, not at all put off by my over-indulgence at that humiliating dinner party, who had advised me, over the course of several visits, as to colour and voluminousness of skirt. In the absence of you, dear Jane, and of any real friend at all, I have become rather fond of Mrs. Littleworth. What I believed to be deafness on our first meeting was only her effort to ensure her husband's participation in the conversation. Indeed, she seemed almost as lonely as I, and we spent many hours discussing fashion here and abroad, quite odd because she herself did not have what one could call a fashionable figure, there being too much of her for fashion to cover except strategically. Still, she seemed to enjoy my prattling on about muslins and silks and in particular those afternoons when the two of us played the card game Twenty-One, newly arrived from France. 'Twould be impossible to tell the girl from the lady with such clapping and laughter echoing about the house. Such a friendship, one between a lady of many years—I would guess her to be in the neighbourhood of forty—and one of few years—I am but eighteen—to be unusual. But friendship is determined by who is nearby. It is sustained by common enthusiasms and deepened by loyalty and affection. Such is the case with Mrs. Littleworth and myself. Oh my, I sound like an old, wise woman, forgive me. I seem to have lost the thread of my story, perhaps my way of avoiding living once again that which awaited me in the ballroom.

I barely noticed Mrs. Littleworth on that night, or anyone else, for there he stood, tall and straight, his dark hair powdered, pulled back, and tied with a band (never a wig for him, such a natural man, though perhaps it was in deference to his guests, these country persons, like my husband, who have forsworn the wearing of wigs forever, muttering as they do something about the French and a tennis court). My colonel had set aside his military uniform for this occasion and was slimly elegant in evening wear tailored to perfection.

Men's breeches—a forbidden subject for such as I or you or any woman of propriety—have never made themselves of interest to me. Mr. Bennet's breeches, for instance, have never been of note. But I must, must continue: my colonel's breeches, banded as they were just below the knees, be still my heart, made a stunning announcement of my colonel's legs, in particular—dare I say—his calves, encased in satin, pulsing with power therein. I know because I dared not look up at him, so God help me, my eyes fastened on—I am small, remember—a point some distance above the calves, to a place that even at my most confessional I will not name. The colonel wore his sword. He would make graceful flourishes with it during the minuet, perhaps with me as his partner. I grew faint with yearning. I must have teetered a bit for I felt Mr. Bennet take my elbow. It was then I noted the young woman standing beside my colonel. She was resplendent in ivory satin and glittering with diamonds about her neck and bosom, her hair sprinkled with smaller but no less precious stones. She was alight with beauty. The world began to spin and once again Mr. Bennet took my elbow and whispered into my ear, "Steady there, old girl." There he goes again! This time as if I were a horse!

I suppose the disaster began then though I chose to ignore warning signs. Firstly, the colonel did not know me. He did not recognize me. The colonel's aide muttered "Mr. and Mrs. Bennet" into his ear and he nodded politely. Although how should he recognize me? I was presented only as Mrs. Bennet, wife of the gentleman who stood next to me smiling that fixed smile he always wears when he is out in society, the smile that says how he detests being wherever it is that I have insisted he appear. I had thought that forcing him into social occasions, small ones such as the little supper for Mr. Collins with only a few guests, would prepare him for more significant events. Apparently not, for here he was, grouchiness personified.

My colonel spoke. To Mr. Bennet! "Ah yes, I believe we are neighbours. My huntsman has spoken to me of what could very well be mutual property." Mr. Bennet sputtered something about enclosure and the colonel said, "Yes, we shall have to discuss this in greater detail. I understand you are not a hunter." He nodded to me and handed me on to the well-lit beauty at his side. "My sister," he announced, "Miss Millar."

My spirits lifted, my head cleared, and my balance returned. His sister! All was not lost. I moved us along the line as quickly as good manners would allow. "Mr. Bennet," I whispered to him, "you need not show your teeth anymore."

He looked relieved, then not, when I said, "Will you have the first dance with your wife?" Silence. "The mother of your children?" He remained unmoved. "The woman you will spend all eternity with?" With a sigh, he bowed, I nodded, and together we made our way past the gaming rooms, where men stood at tables rolling dice, and past the sewing room, where the old ladies, secure in their caps, knitted and chattered to each other or were silent, intent on games of whist. Ah yes, there was Mrs. Littleworth, quite splendid, actually, in her magenta gown whose dips and swoops combined to conceal her unfortunate bosom. Mr. Littleworth, we could see, was already at the buffet table. The magnificent ballroom, resounding with music for the Country Dance, was almost filled with guests, many of them from neighbouring estates, now almost unrecognizable in their finery. We nodded to them and they to us.

At the risk of seeming immodest, I must declare that more than one couple eyed my gown with envy, thus assuring me that I was wise not to offer a distraction from its singularity by way of ornamentation, Miss Millar's bejeweled splendour aside. The ladies of the county, truth be told, looked to be behind the times with respect to fashion: they wore gowns with no panniers, it seemed. Their skirts drooped about their bodies and puddled upon the floor, a most uncelebratory style, I must say. However, my mind was on other matters, and I am certain that, if the next difficulty hadn't occurred, we might almost have enjoyed the music and the dancing, with which Mr. Bennet was not altogether unfamiliar. "No chassé," he warned. "One skip and I leave the floor with or without you." Upon my soul! He is so lacking in adventurousness. He is so cautious. He is so pedestrian. I smiled up at him, pretending for everyone that our union was full of gaiety and mystery. Years had passed since I had practiced my art, but at that moment some part of my earlier self—my fifteen-year-old self—returned to me and I commenced flirting. My eyelashes, glistening with some of Mr. Bennet's shoe polish, fluttered up and down rapidly. Mr. Bennet looked down at me as if I were mad. "Why are you acting the hussy?"

Now, I grant you, my flirting skills may have gotten a bit rusty, but "hussy"? Undaunted, as we entered the dance, arms linked, I pressed his inner arm and lowered my eyes, earning yet another sideways look of suspicion and condemnation. I refused to allow the tears that had gathered in the corners of my eyes to fall, reminding myself of what happens when Mr. Bennet wears his newly polished shoes on a rainy day. I soldiered on, as they say, whispering to myself, "Courage, Marianne." The sound of my name revived me.

My expectation had been that at some point Colonel Millar, recognizing me and remembering our promises of undying love on that singular night alongside the little stream, would tap my husband on the shoulder and beg to become my partner. Mr. Bennet, I had no fear, would accede readily to the colonel's request and I would once again be in the arms of the man to whom I had given my all, and then some. Out of the corner of my eye I could see that he had finished greeting guests and was at that very moment descending the staircase where we would take our rightful turn together. But it was not to be, because of course his partner for the first dance of the evening was his lofty sister. Each time she turned or curtsied or raised her arm she glittered. The whole room glittered, for her jewels were reflected in the chandeliers and, for the briefest of time, we all, countrymen and ladies, sparkled. I must say, we would never see our like again. With each whirl I tossed a flirty glance at the colonel, who, although he appeared intent on his sister-partner, could not have helped but see me, for I spun out just ahead of the rest of the dancers and just a bit wider, my panniers creating a light breeze. Oh yes, I confess that I intended that I stand out from the rest, so that he could not fail to notice my beauty, or certainly my beautiful dress, and recall our night together only a few short years before. Just to make sure, I made an extra-wide turn which brought me close to him, so close my skirt brushed my colonel's ankle. "What are you doing?" Mr. Bennet whispered. I did not answer, simply lowered my lashes (which I must confess lay heavy by now). I had no time to answer, for at this very moment, as Mr. Bennet waited for me to complete yet another turn on the floor, my gown began to come apart.

"Edward, take me away from here," I whispered. "Quickly." He seemed not to understand and continued to dance what looked to me like a silly jig. "Pull me to you, please, I beg of you." Frowning, of course, he did so and knew at once that flight was the only answer.

What his fingers had felt when he clasped me close was the ripping of my gown. At any moment the threads would snap; the bodice would shatter and collapse in sorry splendour about my waist. My corset had burst and the rest would follow in an instant.

So profound a public humiliation is not deserved by even the flightiest of women, the most vainglorious, the most selfish—all of which I confess to being at one time or another, sometimes all at once. I prayed to God above to see me through the coming disaster. I prayed that fate would be kinder than I deserved. I prayed that my colonel would not of a sudden recognize me. I prayed to Edward to make me disappear.

Edward answered my prayer. He understood the disaster at hand, placed his arm about my waist, and with his entire body shielded me and my gown, soon to be in tatters, from public view. Without a skip, without a bow, without a nod of the head, he propelled me from the floor and onto the balcony outside. "Don't move," he said, standing me against a pillar. "I'll get your wrap." At that moment, my husband and my protector became my hero.

I know, dear sister, that I have complained much as to his faults and deficiencies. I know that I have gone to considerable length to avoid his company and his person, even so far as to plead illness when, as you know, I have had nary a day of sickness in my life, unless one counts the lying-in periods, which no one does, motherhood being what it is. And now? It is not too much to say that I owe him my life or by any measure my reputation, in this case one and the same.

We hurried into the chaise and Mr. Bennet ordered the driver to make haste toward Longbourn. I huddled in the corner, wrapped in my cloak, hoping to make myself invisible. Neither of us spoke until the chaise pulled up to the entrance of our house. Coming round to my side, Edward handed me down and whispered in my ear, "You foolish girl." I could not but agree.

Yr Marianne

Ch. 16

In Which I Am at a Loss and We Have Another Caller

Utatur motu animi, qui uti ratione non potest.

"He only employs his passion
who can make no use of his reason."

—CICERO

Mrs. Bennet has been seen only fleetingly, darting about the hallways, her curls matted to her head, her eyes wild, her skin mottled as if from fever. I fear for her sanity. When I have attempted to restrain her mindless perambulations, she shrieks and runs off. The servants, of course, have taken the opportunity afforded them by their mistress's illness to return to their lazy habits of doing nothing. I had taken heart only weeks earlier when Mrs. Bennet seemed to take matters in hand and demanded that they perform their duties properly. Now, because Mrs. Bennet does not appear even for meals, they slouch about the lower floor and about the upstairs and present meals to me fit for themselves, I expect, but certainly not for the master of all they survey. My bed linens are a disgrace; my mother tosses about in her grave.

Mrs. Rummidge, for example, wails loud and long throughout the day as she paces back and forth along the hallway outside Mrs. Bennet's bedroom, cradling one infant, then the other, in her bony arms. "God save your dear mother!" she chants. How this entreaty can help her mistress's condition I shall never know. I order her to desist. She does not. I would order her out of the house if it were not she and only she who looks after the children, their mother having chosen madness over motherhood.

Granted, Mrs. Bennet has good reason to excuse herself from society. That damned ball at Northfield threw into relief her excessive vanity, her o'er-weening pride, and her inability to plan ahead. She was a recipe for failure.

To be sure, she looked, at the beginning of the evening, aglow. My heart leapt at the sight of her descending the staircase in that gown for which I paid more than I have ever paid for any animal of my fields or my barns or pens. But so alight with pleasure and pride was she that I forgave all her extravagances. (Though I will admit that I felt relieved to see that she wore no jewels. God help me if she ever decides to collect.) I was my most gentlemanly self. I held her wrap, she took my arm, and, quite the elegant couple, we stepped up into the chaise (another expense I shall not have to repeat). "You look lovely, my dear," I complimented her. "Thank you, kind sir," she replied, smiling up at me. "Shall we go?" I asked. "Indeed," she answered. There was a lilt in her voice I had not heard since our courting days.

I had not been to Northfield for some years, not since I was a boy. It has stood empty since then until now. The sight of it as we arrived brought back memories of my happy childhood when my mother called on Lady Willoughby there. Lord Willoughby was most often occupied elsewhere, some military excursion I was told, and so, while my mother and Lady Willoughby chatted about children and the events of the day, I had the full run of the estate. I came to know the gamekeeper, the field hands, the Master of the Hounds, and the hounds themselves. Northfield is where I first learned to ride, thanks to the patience of Staunton, the groomsman. Northfield is where I watched the birthing of lambs and of calves and of foals, thanks to the kindness of Bentham, the husbandman. It is from there that I took away the notion of service. How hard, then, it has been to witness in my own home the sloth and the surliness of those in my employ. With the exception of Tom, who cannot be called an actual servant, my household is run by selfish, ignorant, and rudderless nincompoops. In the absence of my wife, she whom I had assumed would put things in order, it will fall upon me to restore the arrangements known to me in my earlier life, the life in which my mother, so effortlessly, commanded loyalty and industriousness from her household staff.

So I was not altogether resistant to attending the party at Northfield. In addition, it might provide an opportunity to speak further with this Colonel Millar concerning our properties which coincide. I have an uneasy feeling that he means to encroach onto my land and will use the absence of enclosure to do so. I shall have to instruct him in the ways of our county, where custom and tradition remain superior to the indignities of legal wrangling. And, with such a beautiful wife by my side, I almost looked forward to the evening.

I might have known that the dancing would take preeminence over practicality. Colonel Millar had no time for conversation. And Mrs. Bennet, strangely, began to pale as we were introduced. Instantly, she demanded that I dance and so, to keep the peace at least in public, I acceded to her request. Her behaviour then became even more peculiar, and if I didn't know of its impossibility, I would have said that she was flirting with me. She began to flutter her eyelids in my direction, press my arm against her side (a first for that, I will say), and nod her quite adorable chin up and then down so frequently as to make my head spin and perhaps hers, too, for she glanced quickly in the direction of the colonel and his sister, then back, and then again. It was like dancing with a small flag caught in the breeze; indeed, at one point she stumbled into Colonel Millar. Perhaps it was my own dizziness that caused me to ignore the disaster about to occur. It required her panicked whispering—"Take me away from here"—to awaken me to the separation of seams in her gown, the gown so costly as to have forced my husbandman to reduce his order for feed for the animals. Of course, I hurried her away from the dancing and out onto the veranda nearby. I ordered her wrap and my chaise and took us both away as quickly as I could. At one point Mrs. Bennet seemed as if she would faint and indeed I suspect she would have had I not been there to hold her upright. She was weaving just as she had when she had gotten tiddly during our dinner party, except that tonight no wine had touched her lips. The thought occurs to me now that Mrs. Rummidge, never far from my wife's side, might well have provided an alcoholic reinforcement. She is capable of anything.

I did my best to comfort Mrs. Bennet on our journey homeward. "Now, now," I murmured, "no one noticed, things can't be that bad, it will all be forgotten by the morrow," but she would have none of my patting or quiet assurances and remained frozen in silence, all light gone from her, a little sparrow huddled into the corner of the chaise. Since then, she has been as you saw her at the first of this diary entry. With one exception.

Late last week, in the late afternoon, she appeared downstairs in her nightdress but with her curls returned to their natural springiness along with some of the rosy colour in her cheeks. The sight of her filled me with hope. As

I moved toward her, she did not turn and run, she did not cry out; instead, I believed she returned a bit of a smile. It was at that moment that a loud knock came at the door.

Surprised, I hastened to open it (no servant having showed herself). There stood Colonel Millar. "Good day," he said. "I thought this might be the opportune time to talk about the enclosure laws that could very well—"

Mrs. Bennet's face, drained of all colour, twisted itself into a prune. She screamed once and fell unconscious to the floor. The colonel made an apology and fled. With the help of Mrs. Rummidge, who heard the commotion from above and hastened down, we carried my poor Marianne up to bed, where she remains.

I am left to wonder who this woman is. She is not a wife, she is barely a mother to my children, she is not by any means the mistress of my house; and yet, something in me warms to her and wishes for her warmth in return. She is but a girl. Perhaps time will bring forth the woman. I would that it were sooner than later.

Ch. 17

July at Longbourn

Dear Sister,

I have let the whole of June escape and have barely the strength to resume my correspondence now in the sensuous languors of summer. I spend many afternoons, as I spend this one, sitting beneath the linden, listening to the murmurs of innumerable bees, their sound like distant music. Mr. Bennet comes by on occasion to amuse me with tales of farm life, as for instance, those regarding Tom, who delights in the warm weather.

"Well, now, Mrs. Bennet," my husband said only minutes ago, attempting Tom's country speech, "I finished my hayrick in most excellent fashion, and was able to cut all my hay in five days." I would add that Tom is a most able-bodied farmer while my husband is not, and so, try as I will to pretend that I am entertained, my eyes and the downturn of my mouth give me away. I am not amused.

I pity my husband. It is not his fault that I am sad; after all, it is his heroics that saved me from total and complete humiliation before the entire county at the colonel's ball. And he could not know the effect that Colonel Millar's sudden appearance on our doorstep would have on me. But oh, Jane, picture me in my dressing gown, my hair awry, not covered by a cap, my feet unshod. I was barefoot! In the vestibule of my own home, there was I, mistress of Longbourn, looking for all the world like a madwoman unfit for human company, as indeed I was. What recourse did I have then but to faint dead away. Pretense was impossible, oblivion was not.

My contemplation in solitude has brought me to this: I must put away foolish notions of the colonel. I must fasten on my life as a wife and mother. I must set aside my daydreams and attend to my responsibilities. It is no less than my husband deserves. To be sure, he is not and never can be my heart's desire. He can never replace my colonel in my affections. But he seems, for all that, a decent man who means no harm. I have not been worthy of him.

It is my misfortune to end this letter with the news that, once again, I am with child. It is no wonder that my gown split. Pray that I will deliver a son.

Yr sister,
Marianne

Ch. 18

Quae venit indigne poena dolenda venit.

"We are entitled to complain of a punishment that we have not deserved."

—OVID

What is my sin? What wrong have I done, what crime have I committed to deserve the dull stares or, worse, the weeping that seems as if it would consume my wife? I have exhausted myself with searching for a sensible argument that would explain such behaviour, but none comes. I will leave her to her misery. Only she can heal herself. So I earnestly pray.

At the risk of seeming an unfeeling lout, I will add to

my complaints one other: Mrs. Bennet is growing stouter by the day. And no wonder. The only company she seeks out is the cook's and often I find her furtively cramming sweets into her mouth. Means she this balm to soothe her fevered brow? Another damnable perplexity.

Ch. 19

A Terrible Accident

Late at night, a terrible cry. I raced to her bedroom door, flung it open, and looked on in horror at the bedclothes red with blood. Marianne raised herself from the pillows and in a voice from the depths of hell said, “You have your son, and he is dead!”

I cannot go on. Forgive me.

Ch. 20

Mid-July at Longbourn

Dearest Jane,

You are the only one to whom I can express the anguish I feel over the death of my son. I share my grief with you as I trust you will share yours with me. The fine and honest man who was your husband is gone from you as is my little boy from me, and now you and I are alone. How fortunate you were to have had his good company for these past years. I hope and pray that his long illness prepared you for the end. Would that I had had even a little time to give my son life.

I write this from my bed. My writing desk was once a small table whose legs Mr. Bennet has cut down so as to make a tray which straddles my now empty and useless womb. Although it was our tenant Tom who did the carpentry, it was Mr. Bennet himself whose thoughtfulness made this letter possible. And I, shameful creature that I am, could not carry to term the child that would have perfected his happiness. I am of no worth.

I have not risen from this bed for many a day, almost fourteen now. I have no plans to do so. The grief of losing our son lies on me like a stone and renders me incapable of resuming household duties or the mothering of my two daughters. I have asked Mrs. Rummidge to keep them from me, for seeing them would serve to remind me that while they are full of life and in good spirits, their little brother lies beneath the earth. My first visit to the outside world, should there be a first visit, will be to the family cemetery next to our chapel, the chapel where my daughters were christened, the chapel you no doubt remember well, the chapel my little boy will never see.

I did attend the service which laid him to rest, but I remember little of it, only that Mr. Bennet held me upright once again and that my black veil hid me from view and from viewing. I doubt that I could have been comforted by your presence or by the ministrations of anyone. Even now my tears, unbidden, rush into my eyes and spill onto my cheeks; I am a torrent of grief. I have forbidden anyone to come near me, no one. I eat a little of what Cook fixes for me; I care not if I live or die. Mrs. Rummidge delivers to me a cup of tea every so often, laced with, I suspect, an infusion of laudanum, enough to stanch my tears and return me to the arms of Morpheus. I am grateful. His casket was so small.

It would not do for you to visit us now. I am too full of sorrow and would only burden you further with my grief. Until we meet, know that I share your grief for the loss of your dear husband. Grieving widows, grieving mothers, the world seems full of nothing else. By what right are our loved ones taken from us? I would curse the answer if ever the forces that live so beyond our powers would show themselves. Cowards all, to heap sorrow upon sorrow upon women too weak and ignorant to fight back. My tears are now of anger.

Yr sister,
Marianne

Ch. 21

Summer's End

Dear Sister,

Mr. Bennet has insisted that I rouse myself and attend with him the autumn festival held each year in our village. At first, I refused his invitation, but then he caught my eye and I realized that grief was not mine alone. I do not believe that he has trimmed his whiskers or straightened his neck cloth or paid much attention at all to his general cleanliness. "Mr. Bennet," I said, "you are odoriferous. Please avail yourself of the opportunity to bathe yourself." I did not mean to sound so harsh, but he spoke not a word, just tucked his chin into his collar and started for the door. "Edward," I said more softly, "thank you for this most agreeable little writing desk you have made for me." He looked up shyly, and suddenly I could see the boy he once was.

"My pleasure, my dear," he answered. He bowed slightly. "And now I shall leave you to your rest."

"Don't go quite yet," I said. I patted the edge of the bed. "Sit with me here for a bit."

I believe he feared I might have a change of heart, for he almost leapt across the room to do my bidding, and before either of us knew it, we were chatting as if we were a longtime married couple. "Tell me how the household is managing in my absence," I said and added, "Not that the household ran all that smoothly when I was in charge. Oh, Edward, was I ever in charge? Tell me true."

Good gracious, didn't he smile, then turned earnest. "Well, my dear, you were new to housekeeping and to having so serious a charge over people who themselves were no great gift to the servant class. I'm not sure how they came to Longbourn or even who hired them."

"It was my responsibility," I answered. "I relied overly on Mrs. Rummidge's recommendations. But worse, I paid little attention to how they carried out their duties or even if they carried them out at all. I shall endeavour to make some changes in that regard once I am back on my feet." Without warning, I felt the tears begin. "Oh, Edward, I cannot forget the horror of that night and the loss of our infant son. I have wronged you."

He took my hand. "Now, now, Marianne," he said,

"more of that another time. Please, just for now, dry your tears. I have brought you an invitation." He rushed on. "The autumn festival we spoke about will be held in the village Sunday next. I thought that perhaps the two of us might wander down and enjoy the festivities of the day. We might even take our children. I believe that the appearance of our little family would gladden the hearts of many. It may please you to know that many have shared in your grief. Many have asked daily about your recovery, your health, and sent their good wishes to you. Mrs. Littleworth, for one, has called daily to enquire as to your progress. She appears to have a genuine fondness for you."

All this took me by surprise, and I feared the return of tears. It never occurred to me that I was in the least an object of sympathy—curiosity perhaps, but not sympathy. Edward's words touched me. "I shall do my best to make myself presentable, but I cannot promise to be as you or Mrs. Littleworth wishes. I may never be that woman, ever. But I will attend the festival on your arm. I accept your kind invitation."

"The warm sun awaits you," he said, "and with a happy heart, I take my leave." He bowed and as he backed his way out the door, he smiled broadly. "I am happy to see that you are regaining your health," he said. "And your powers of speech."

Dear Jane, I do not look forward to a silly fair where people cavort in the sunshine and are happy. I do not want to go. But I must. It is time. This festival shall begin my penance. I did not utter a falsehood when I told Mr. Bennet that I had wronged him. I have lost his son and I have given him a daughter not his and I have disgraced him at the ball. Were he to face those truths, even one of them, he would have the right to toss me into the streets where some would say I belong. Not only that, dear sister, for although my dear child is gone now these three weeks, a weight remains on my spirit that time has not shaken off. Will it ever be thus? The effort is mine to commence. Pray for me.

Marianne

Ch. 22

In Which We Regain Respectability and Coincidence Threatens

Abducendus etiam non nunquam animus est ad alia studia, sollicitudines, curas, negotia; loci denique mutatione, tanquam aegroti non convalescentes saepe curandus est.

"The mind is sometimes to be diverted to other studies . . . by change of place, as sick persons who do not recover are ordered change of air."

—CICERO

I find September a most agreeable month, the end of the gentleness of summer yet before the cruelties of winter begin. It celebrates the end of harvest, which, according to

Tom, was most successful despite the drought that threatened in July. Today the paths of the village are lined with farm families offering their late-summer wares: apples firm and rosy, walnuts, the gourds of pumpkin and squash. I was heartened to see Cook amongst the crowd weighing apples and squashes in her hands, eyeing beets and radishes and carrots. Emily, the scullery maid, followed along behind her, stumbling as Cook filled her basket with provisions for the months to come. I smiled, as did Mrs. Bennet, at Cook's playing the grand lady, nose in the air, skirts billowing as she strode along the paths, arms free of baskets, her servant, the beast of burden, trailing behind.

"My good man," we heard her say to a vendor, "my perusals have been such that your cabbages win over all. Be so good as to fill my servant's basket with several of those and an armful of your onions as well. Summer squash still firm, is it?" "But Mrs. Waters," Emily complained, "I cannot carry so heavy a load." "You are paid to do my bidding," Cook sniffed. "And when will that be?" murmured Emily.

"O husband," said Mrs. Bennet, "oughtn't we to intervene? Emily is quite correct."

Startled by the sound of "husband," I replied, "They will do quite well without us. Simply nod as we walk by." I was pleased to see Cook attending to foodstuffs here. There has been a change in the servants that seemed to begin with Mrs. Bennet's misfortune. They have expressed concern that seems genuine and have hurried about their chores without the scolding of Mrs. Rummidge, in itself an ear-splitting unpleasantness.

We passed many of our neighbours as we strolled, I pushing Jane and Elizabeth in their carriage, Mrs. Bennet close by my side. With each pause and exchange of pleasantries, Elizabeth attempted to climb out of the perambulator. We were not in the least surprised. Each day she seems more determined to meet life on her own terms. Sitting in a carriage is not one of them. Jane, on the other hand, is quite content to smile up at those who chuck her under the chin and google silly words at her. Elizabeth is close to perfecting a scowl. The contrast in their characters was no more in evidence than when Mr. and Mrs. Littleworth stopped to bid welcome to us all. As Mr. Littleworth made buzzing noises and waggled his finger ever closer to the children, Jane gurgled her delight. Elizabeth tried to beat his finger away with her tiny fists and pinched her little face into a red ball of fury. Fortunately, Mrs. Littleworth interceded and reached for his finger before it reached Elizabeth's nose. "Careful, my dear. This one shows signs of willfulness," she said approvingly.

Mrs. Bennet looked on. For too long she has refused the company of her children and so it was good to see that their winning ways—Jane's at any rate—were pleasing to her. She said to Mrs. Littleworth, "My husband has told me of your kindness during my recent illness. Allow me to offer my deepest gratitude."

"Well, my dear," Mrs. Littleworth said, "tragedy befalls

us one and all"—here I could swear she gestured toward Mr. Littleworth—"and it has come to you far too early. I have been giving some thought as to how we might brighten your days. I shall call on you soon. Good day for now."

And off they went, Mr. Littleworth mumbling something about being late for tea.

And then, to my surprise, along came Colonel Millar, his beautiful sister at his side. I did not recollect that he was such a tall person, nor she. "Good afternoon," the colonel said. His sister nodded.

"Good afternoon to you," I answered. "I would not have expected to see you here in this month of autumn. London must beckon."

Miss Millar nodded in agreement and the colonel said, "We are savouring our final days in the country before the start of the season. Shortly, we will ready ourselves during a few weeks in Bath. Then it's off to London."

"Yes," said the beauteous Miss Millar. "Once the season is upon us we barely have time for breath. Parties and banquets and balls, you know, each more splendid than the one before." She smiled down from her considerable height at Mrs. Bennet. "I have warned my dressmaker that her days and nights belong to me. It would be most unfortunate should a gown separate from itself during the dancing, which I find utterly exhausting but scintillating nonetheless. Don't you agree?"

Mrs. Bennet grew pale.

That cursed woman. How dare she so much as suggest knowledge of the catastrophe that befell us at Northfield those long months ago!

The colonel stepped up to fill the silence. "See here, Bennet," he said to me. "When are we two going to sit down and discuss our common properties? I suggest we meet within a fortnight. I'll send my man with dates and times. I'm sure you agree with me that this fencing of properties is a good thing." "Perhaps on further introspection, you will agree that it is not," I returned. Colonel Millar turned to the perambulator. "Well, now, whom do we have here?" He leaned down and took little Jane's hand. "She is already a beauty." He turned to Mrs. Bennet and paused a bit longer than I would have liked. "She resembles her lovely mother." He bowed much lower and much longer than I thought necessary, just as I thought his holding her hand pushed against the boundary of polite behaviour. What was this fellow up to?

"Come, brother," said the odious sister. "We must be off." With all the haughtiness one might expect of a royal personage, she turned abruptly, seized her brother's arm, and proceeded in a direction opposite of ours. It was clear to me, at least, that the colonel was not quite so eager to leave the scene. He fastened his glance on my wife as long as possible, until his sister spoke to him—no doubt a reprimand—and he turned away.

Indeed, you must be off, I thought, and not a moment too soon. All colour had left Mrs. Bennet's face, and she clung to the children's carriage as if she would fall. What is this with fainting and deathly pallor and loss of speech? She who had so delighted me with her return to good health seemed to have returned to invalidism. As I think of it, I cannot help but wonder if this colonel is in some way connected to her spells: he has, after all, been present at three of her four swoons. But then I imagine that if I were to put 2 and 2 together I would get 5. Nothing about my wife makes sense. Perhaps a change of scene is due.

Ch. 23

September at Longbourn

Dear Jane,

I have grown so stout as to have forsworn the wearing of any corset at all, at least within the confines of my home. For reasons unknown I crave sweets and am at Cook day and night for treacle on bread slathered with butter. Even writing this brings pangs of starvation. All one need do is see my reflection in the looking glass to know that I am well fed, overly fed one might say. I avoid reflections of myself in any form, and were it not for the necessity of presenting myself in public, my plumpness would remain a secret even to myself. I cannot understand my intense desire for sugars and creams and butters. Were it not that my poor dear little Edward was placed so recently in his grave, I might suspect another child within me. I am the right size, heaven knows. But Edward has not been with me these many months now so I am hopeful that my own restraint will return me once again to the slimness of my youth.

The autumn festival was pleasant enough or would have been had I not had to bind myself into my largest corset so as to appear as respectable as Mr. Bennet would have me. He has become something of a family man, not so dedicated to studies in his library as once he was. He has shown himself solicitous of my health and pleased with my return to good health, or so he believes. Often, I have seen him out my window, either Elizabeth or Jane on his shoulders, tramping along the path and into the meadows. "I shall teach my daughters to fish," he has told me, "once the trout begin jumping again in our stream." The three of them arouse in me feelings I thought were lost forever. I desired to join their happy trio, and so off to the festival we went, all of us clad in our mourning clothes.

Such respectability had not truly been known to me up to that point in my life. Heretofore I had been nurturing children or entertaining romantic notions of the man whom I would make my king. For the first time since my marriage to Edward I felt a contentment, even a bit of pride, in the picture we must have painted for the villagers and our neighbours as the two of us, our children in tow, strolled the paths of the village. Had I not been so confined by my corset, I might have experienced true happiness.

At the end of the village, where town gives way to meadow, maidens of the village danced to the fiddle and the flute, skirts swirling about their ankles, indeed showing more than just their ankles as the music grew louder and faster. Soon they were joined by the young lads of the town, who swung them round so that their cheeks grew rosy and their breath came faster until the tune ended. Some girls looked as if they might fall to the ground were it not that the lads caught hold of them tight as anyone could wish. I was reminded of our girlhood—yours and mine—when we danced in the village square around the maypole. Do you recall Ned Lonergan sweeping me up as I loosed myself from the garlands and spinning me round till I feared to lose myself? You cried, "Ned, Ned! Keep care of her!" and reached out your hand to stop him. To no avail, none at all. Ah, the sweetness of it all! And now, here I am, going on nineteen, my youth spent, and fat as a cow.

To make matters as bad as they could possibly be, I espied a short distance away Colonel Millar talking most animatedly with Mrs. Littleworth, his very slim sister some steps behind and looking very bored. Mrs. Littleworth bowed and returned to the direction from which she had come. I was thankful; at least I would not have to suffer her nosiness. However, Colonel Millar and sister continued to advance.

I became mute.

Miss Millar babbled on about taking the waters in Bath and the upcoming London season, her head swaying this way and that upon her swan-like neck. Just when I had concealed most of my bulk and my mourning dress behind Mr. Bennet—once again my protector and shield—I heard her say, ". . . most unfortunate should a gown separate from itself during the dancing." My heart plummeted. The disaster that had befallen me at the ball had not gone unnoticed. I had not escaped public scrutiny and this dreadful woman's ridicule. The world spun about me, though not in the happy way it had on our village green. It was only the babies' carriage I grasped that kept me upright. I must admit that Mr. Bennet, for good reason, may very well have tired of holding me up, especially now that I have added excess poundage.

The colonel saved me. How brilliantly tall he was there in his country clothes, although I could not bring myself to look much beyond his boots, their rich leather contouring his, dare I say, well-turned calves. Forgive me, Jane, I can only hope that the writing of these things will cure me of the illness—for yes, my passion for this man had come upon me once again and threatened my newfound contentment. I do not recall what he said, only that it drew attention away from his impolite sister and the target of her disdain, myself.

I had almost regained my composure when, of a sudden, the colonel bent down and placed his hand on little Jane's head, a caress so right and true as I have never seen. "She is already a beauty," he said, and then, "She resembles her lovely mother." He looked directly into my eyes and, Jane,

I swear I saw recognition in his. I yearned to burst out with "She resembles her father. She resembles you, my dear colonel." He moved his hand, then, from her head down along the contours of her face and took her chin in his hand. "You are a sweet one." Jane gazed up at him, her blue eyes bright with happiness, and answered with her most delicious baby chuckle.

His sister called him away, and my world turned on its head. "There she goes again," I could hear Mr. Bennet say, though this time I caught myself from sinking to the ground beneath me.

I do not remember our walk back home or Elizabeth's squalling to be let out of her carriage or Mr. Bennet's look of confusion or little Jane's eyes filling with tears; Mr. Bennet apprised me of all this as, safe within Longbourn, we two stood at the window and watched the bonfire from the village light up the night sky. "Whatever is dead will go up in flames; the earth will begin her sleep to ready itself for new growth come spring," Mr. Bennet said. I said not a word but I thought, Those are the flames of hell in which my soul shall perish.

By morning my spirits had risen somewhat, and I received Mrs. Littleworth in as agreeable a mood as had been mine for many weeks. And what a visit it turned out to be! First off, Mrs. Littleworth seems not the person who dined with us during Mr. Collins's visit where she seemed silly and definitely addled. Perhaps that was the persona she adopted in the presence of her husband, who himself seemed more than a little befuddled. I cannot know for certain; all I can know is that during this momentous visit she was the picture of uprightness and clear-headedness. But oh, I cannot hold off any longer: Mrs. Littleworth has invited me to accompany her to Bath! "A visit to a place unfamiliar to you, sans children, sans husband, is just what you need," she said. "You have too long been morose. A change of scene, that will do the trick." I do not know what she means by sans husband and children, but "A change of scene" spoke to me at once. She made as if to leave, then said, "Do what you must to gain your husband's consent. I will assure mine that my intention is to introduce you to Society. He is too suspicious of me, accusing me of preferring the gambling halls to the baths. Your presence will allay his concerns." She winked. "We leave for Bath on Monday next."

"Introduce me to Society." Oh, if only she knew what that meant to me. Sooner than I could have new gowns made I would breathe the air of my colonel; I would, surely, find myself in his company; I will not turn faint and tongue-tied. I will be a proper lady of Bath, come to take the air and enjoy the company of persons yet unknown and of one person, very much known, my one true love. It is as if fate has given me a second, perhaps a third, chance to turn my life aright.

And so, dear sister, I seduced my husband. Bedecked, bedizened, and be-ribboned, I made my way that night to Mr. Bennet's bedchamber. I was quite uncertain as to how to proceed. After all, I had had only one experience of seduction, that being the single night when my colonel took my virginity and left me only memories, with of course little Jane to renew them. Thus, in the absence of experience I determined to make use of my memories in the hope that my husband would give me leave to make the journey to Bath.

Forgive me, dear sister, for what will seem an indelicacy in this transcription, my apology precedes presentation. I can offer as an excuse only my desperation to flee from this house, from my husband, my children and, I prayed, my passion for this man, Colonel Millar, whose reappearance in my life has served to inflame me once again and whose disappearance from my heart I hope a fortnight in Bath will ensure. You may think, dear Jane, that seduction is an odd way to overcome passion, but seduction was the only means available to me, or so Mrs. Rummidge led me to believe.

To say that my appearance in Mr. Bennet's bedchamber was a surprise is an understatement of the first order. I held the lamp in such a way that its light made a halo about my head and, indeed, Mr. Bennet thought me at first an apparition. "Who goes there?" he called out and started up from his pillow. "It is only I, your wife," I whispered just loudly enough to be heard and softly enough to soothe. "Please, husband, may I enter?" I lowered the lantern to my nightdress, so that it would illuminate the outline of my breasts. "I find myself quite unexpectedly at a loss this night and afraid of night terrors. I would that your companionship can dispel such fears. But, kind sir, I await your permission before I cross your threshold." I tossed my uncapped curls prettily. What a vixen, I!

"I see you have already crossed the threshold," said Mr. Bennet, "and in a most charming manner. Pray, come closer." I did as he asked. "Set down your lamp," he said. "One would hate to see your lovely nightdress set afire." I did as he asked. "And settle yourself here." He patted the side of his bed. I joined him there, situating the folds of my nightdress so that they clung to the curves of my body.

Do you see, dear Jane, that without so much as a thought, men seek control of any event in which they find themselves? And they do so, if not through physical force, then by power of speech, which shows itself when they bellow orders to those about them. A poor sort of power, if you ask me. Still, what recourse do we poor women have? Now was not the time, certainly, to protest or to offer argument. Now was the time to summon our ultimate weapon, our bodies. And here I defer to Mrs. Rummidge.

I take nothing for true from the prattle of Mrs. Rummidge. There is nothing she has not experienced, so she says, and she advises me and anyone within hearing on the proper way of giving birth, on avoiding pregnancy altogether, on child-rearing, mothering, fathering, schooling, and on behaviour of both children and adults as befits those born into the gentry. I learned early on to turn a deaf ear to her sermons and to distrust her claims of securing successive husbands for the benefit of the numerous children she insists she has borne without a whimper. I suspect that in fact she is a spinster whose fantasy life has enriched the parched nature of her actual life. Here I pause to remark on that particular commonality shared by we two. For has not that been true of my own life? And so I do not shut my ears to her on all occasions. A good thing, too, for one such sermon will serve me well this night. I summon up her advice on woman's ultimate weapon:

"Now, dearie," she began. I sighed my exasperation. Nothing I have been able to say will convince her that "dearie" is an improper means of addressing one's superior. If separation between classes exists—and I have no doubt that it does—I do not believe that Mrs. Rummidge is aware of it. "We women," she declared, seating herself heavily onto the damask of my armchair, "weak and silly as we are, find ourselves at the mercy of men, who, so they would have us believe, are strong and wise, invincible in both word and deed." With that, my attention belonged to her, for such has my experience taught me. "What, then, are we to do to maintain our position in the family, in the household, and in the society at large? Let us begin with family, no, with husbands. The rest will follow." She took a deep breath and said, "Mind what I say now." Her voice deepened and became silky soft. "We have at our disposal one weapon that makes us invincible: our bodies." I gasped and made as if to leave the room; such outlandish notions were most improper. "No, madam," she said, "stay. Do not turn away, do not lower your eyes, for what I say is the truth." I resumed my seat on the bed, though I would have preferred to fling myself into my chair, which sadly was already occupied. Instantly, Mrs. Rummidge rose and rushed to bar the door. As she did, I hurried to take my rightful place on my chair, where I planned to feign a small swoon, but she was too quick for me. Leaning forward, she continued, more loudly this time: "Men grow mad for our bodies. Nothing else—not their horses, their dogs, their gold, their sport—can compete with the body of a woman. A man will go to any lengths to bed a woman, and not just a woman of his society, but women who are the lowest of the low. And, though we have been taught otherwise, it is not the perfections of body, it is not the youth and beauty of body, it is that we have a body at all. They don't much mind how scented we are, how clean we have made ourselves, how prettily we have dressed ourselves. No, it is the fact of our bodies that turns men into slaves. Our minds, our manners count for naught. All we need do is show up and the rumblings commence."

Well, this would certainly explain Mr. Bennet's pursuit of me upstairs, downstairs, and in my lady's chamber. "Pray, continue," I urged, though as I gazed at poor Mrs. Rummidge's arms like sticks and cheeks shrunken into her head, I could not but wonder if what she was preaching applied to her as well or if this was merely another of her fantasies.

"To bend them to our will," she went on, "we need only

learn how best to use the body." This, I gathered, would be the most important part of Mrs. Rummidge's sermon, for she pointed her finger into the air. "Less is more, certainly at the beginning. Allow him just a peek at what you have in store." I recalled Mrs. Littleworth's breast bobbing from her gown. Surely such a sight would not serve to entice anyone. As if she were reading my thoughts, Mrs. Rummidge added, "Of course, if what they see is smooth and pliant, the contest will proceed more quickly. Complete disrobing need never occur but if it does, make certain it occurs later than sooner. Some men, by the way, like to help."

Here I held up my hand. "Enough for now," I said. Any more of her advice and I would have fainted dead away.

"All right, lovey," she answered and hurried off to the nursery. I have never known anyone but Mrs. Rummidge to have the last word.

And so it was that there in my husband's bedchamber, perched on the edge of the bed, I began the long process of disrobing. I recalled my colonel's gentle touch—and Mrs. Rummidge's sermon—and slipped my shoulder free. I could see that Mr. Bennet's rumblings had commenced.

Ch. 24

Sensus, o superi, sensus.

"The senses, O ye gods, the senses."

—MONTAIGNE

I cannot write what I feel, so unaccustomed am I to feeling. Yet feeling threatens to overwhelm me, to overpower reason and good sense and judgement. It is my earnest hope that writing however much of experience I can bear to record might restore the faculties that have stood me in such good stead. Until now.

Oh, do not misunderstand. I have not been devoid of feeling. I have great affection for my dogs and an even greater affection for my daughters, albeit they are daughters and not sons. I suppose I could count as feelings when, as a youth, I passed some evenings at Mrs. Brown's London establishment. And I suppose that, in the early days of my marriage, my feelings—well, perhaps they got a bit out of hand. Still, as I have sworn to be truthful, I am forced to admit that yes, in the beginning my feelings were lustful.

There, I have told the worst. And see what has happened: my grammar has been thrown into torment. My Latin master, Mr. Winthrop, bless his departed soul, could very well be spinning in his grave. But I must soldier on. As I believe Cervantes said, "Faint heart ne'er won fair lady"—or anything else, I might add. Thus, I gird my loins and advance.

My wife—she who bore my children, dear girls albeit girls, she who resisted my every advance, she who turned away from me at every opportunity, who grew tipsy at the dinner table, who once—and once only—seemed to welcome my attentions and then most likely on account of an over-abundance of wine—this very woman came to me of her own free will and proceeded to seize the advantage—provided by my astonishment—and overpower me.

Allow me to explain; perhaps then I will understand: My wife and daughters and I had passed a pleasant afternoon in the village, enjoying the sights and sounds of the autumn festival. It was our first outing since the death of our little boy, and I was hopeful that my wife would be cheered by the throngs of people and the gaily decorated stands filled with the bounty of the earth. And so she seemed, at least until that Colonel Millar and his blasted sister happened along. Miss Millar made reference to Marianne's misfortune at the ball and, lord, didn't my wife look as if she would faint again. Fortunately she steadied herself, and we returned home none the worse for wear. That infernal woman, Miss Millar, using her beauty and her position to bring insult to those less fortunate. Not that Marianne is not beautiful, just that she outweighs Miss Millar by several stone, at least at the moment. Really, it is merely the contrast here that causes me to remark on any such nonsense at all. I tried to explain all this to Marianne, but she would have none of it and carried on at length through the entirety of the daylight hours that remained.

And then, the very next night, long past the hour when children and servants were abed, she entered my room—and here yet another confession: we have never shared a sleeping chamber—at her insistence, mind you, certainly not mine. I accepted this marital slight out of politeness, out of concern that she be happy here at Longbourn. This did not appear to happen. And then came her lying-in periods—rather lengthy I thought, despite Mrs. Rummidge's assurances to the contrary—and then headaches and the like, those discomforts of womanhood that seemed to last forever. "O la!" she exclaimed more than once. "My constitution has never been so fragile! Please remain a safe distance from me." That distance seemed to grow with each passing month—she was again with child—when tragedy struck. She miscarried my only son. I must not return to the horror of that night even in memory; suffice it to say that the elemental scene of blood and screams caused me to forswear forever intimacy of any sort with this woman. I kept to my promise, that is until the very night under examination, the night she entered my chamber alone, candle aloft.

"Who goes there?" I called out and started up from my pillow. "It is only I, your wife," she whispered softly. "Please, husband, may I enter?" She lowered the lantern to her nightdress, where it illuminated the outline of her breasts. "I find myself quite unexpectedly at a loss this night and afraid of night terrors. I would that your companionship can dispel such fears. But, kind sir, I await your permission before I cross your threshold." She tossed her uncapped curls prettily, not at all as she tossed her curls most of the time, that being when she was angry.

"I see you have already crossed the threshold," I said, "and in a most charming manner. Pray, come closer." She did. "Set down your lamp," I commanded. "One would hate to see your lovely nightdress set afire." She did. "And settle yourself here." I patted the side of the bed. She obeyed, gathering her nightdress about the supple lines of her body.

As you can tell, I was in complete command at this point. My wife was more obedient, more compliant than I had ever seen her. This would be the beginning of a true marriage. Of this I felt certain.

And then she proceeded to unclothe herself. And I was lost. She had set the candle on the table next to the bed so that its light flickered over her as first she slipped one shoulder from the nightgown and then the other. Before I could advise her of the inadvisability of such behaviour, there she was, naked to the waist. I was vanquished. Her breasts—plumper than when we married, tipped with nipples as rosy as any I had ever seen, admittedly few, but still—were more beautiful than any Aphrodite in any book, even in those books I kept hidden, reserved as they were for special times. “Lie back,” she ordered. I obeyed. Could this be but a dream? And then she kissed me. Now where, I asked myself, did she learn to do that? “Be still,” she ordered. I obeyed and murmured, “I am your slave.”

Do you not see how round-about, how topsy-turvy this all is? I am master of Longbourn and all that reside herein. I am husband, father. I am the patriarch. But I risked it all that one night when reason fled and passion took its place.

Memory refuses me entry to the rest of the night. I can recall only her mouth on every part of my body, her hands on parts of me she had heretofore refused even to look at, her hair as it swept my chest, her squeals of delight when at last I entered her. Afterward, we lay close together, exhausted by delight. And there we lay until morning.

Now she is gone to Bath and I remain here, devastated by my longing for the woman who showed herself to me for the first—and only—time that night.

I shall use her absence to restore strong will and discipline in myself. This yearning is most unmanly.

Ch. 25

At Bath

Dear Jane,

"First, we must get you properly dressed. Take off that dreadful mourning garb." This is what Mrs. Littleworth said to me immediately as we arrived at the house she had taken in Laura Place. A most impressive address! And a most impressive house! With two drawing rooms! For receiving and entertaining guests! My goodness, there is enough room for a ball!

But I must tell you something of our arrival here. Such a change from country life! As we drove through the long course of streets, the calls of muffin men and milkmen, the rumble of carts and drays, the clattering of clogs necessary for walking the muddy streets—everything all about makes noise. The excitement of it was pleasing to me; I had been too long confined. Here I would not rest in my rooms or fret over servants or children. Here I would not concern myself with my husband, his deficiencies and, on occasion, his kindness. Here I would discover my own true self. I would be once again a girl. The woman, if ever she existed, remained far behind, in Longbourn. Bath would bring to life a new woman, the woman I was meant to be.

And so, thanks to the miracles wrought by Mrs. Littleworth's dressmaker, I put behind me the drabness of mourning and stuffed myself into the latest fashions of Bath, the silks and the muslins, the cashmere, fabrics that caused me to bury my face in them and partake of their richness. I say "stuffed" because I have not yet been successful in returning to my youthful slimness. I am certain, however, that all the activities planned for me by Mrs. Littleworth will replace my hunger for foods not designed for holding back the stone. In addition, the kitchen here is nowhere in view, and I do not intend to search for it. One look at Mrs. Littleworth's chins and the folds of her belly, not much disguised by the yards of silk and linen that flow about her person, and I can see my future. If I am not careful. And I will be careful. In all things.

This afternoon we will call on acquaintances of Mrs.

Littleworth. Afternoon calls are frequent, she informs me, and a chief source of amusement here in Bath. I wonder how she will introduce me. Who will I be?

Yrs with affection,
Marianne

Ch. 26

Vivet, et est vitae nescius ipse suae.

"He lives, but does not know he is alive."

—OVID

No word from Marianne during the whole time she has spent away from home. Mr. Littleworth dropped by Tuesday last to inform me that the ladies—his and mine—had arrived safely.

"Most likely the last," he announced.

"The last what?" I enquired.

"The last visit to Bath," he said. "Regina's health is her primary concern. She has determined that taking a house in Bath will cure her." He coughed. "The waters, you know."

"So do you expect her to remain in Bath for a lengthy period?"

"No," said Mr. Littleworth. "Once she discovers that the waters taste like sulfur and have no curative powers whatsoever she will hurry home where she can command the entirety of the household staff to do her bidding. No, she will leave Bath, I anticipate, within the next fortnight." He harrumphed. "I would have said most likely the last fortnight, but that fortnight has passed so most likely the last fortnight will have to wait until it gets here. That's when our ladies will return."

I could make little sense out of what he was saying and so I broached the topic that continued to trouble me, that being my property rights and the colonel's encroachment onto my property. "What," I asked Mr. Littleworth, "have you done to secure your boundaries? I see you have multiple hedges. Do they serve to keep others out? Will you need further enclosure? Colonel Millar seems to believe that all properties are ripe for his hunting."

"I see that Northfield is closed up again," he said. "The fair Miss Millar has departed the scene in favour of the scene in London. When I enquired about Colonel Millar, she murmured something about his spending a bit of time elsewhere before joining her in London. Odd that," he continued. "One rarely sees one without the other. Which means nothing, for when I saw her last at Northfield, she was not accompanied by her brother who may not have been there at all or perhaps was and perhaps for the last time. Time for tea. Good day."

All hopes for advice or counsel or conversation dashed,

I left the premises and fastened my mind onto Mr. Littleworth's assurance that our wives would return within a fortnight, perhaps even sooner. After all, he could have predicted a stay of many fortnights hence, sending me into yet another slough of despond. As resolute as I had been to reclaim my manliness, I must admit to failure in this regard. I took whatever steps were available to me. I visited Tom regularly, for instance, and engaged him in fruitful conversation about the coming winter, about the hunt that would soon transpire across his small acreage and my large one, and we agreed that the future in which hunters were forbidden to ride roughshod wherever they pleased was unfortunately far away. Like Marianne.

I enjoyed talking to Tom. He seems a level-headed fellow, content with his station in life and with his family. Tom's eldest daughter, Mathilda, now almost seventeen, continued to please my eye. I write this because I wish to note that in my wife's absence, I did not lose my singularity, that quality which distinguishes man from woman. No, I was quite able to stir myself into a firmness which could do battle with whoever appeared on the horizon. Mathilda, I must say, is wise beyond her years, for she arranged to be absent as often as was possible during my visits to her father's farm. Uneducated in the ways of proper society, she knew by instinct of the inappropriateness of her attraction to me. And so she pretended, when she was present, not to notice me. In fact, several times she stumbled over my foot on her way to and from the barn; truly, it was as if I didn't exist. Clever girl.

But I could not spend all my free hours in the company of a tenant farmer and his family. So I found myself looking for companionship from my daughters. They are a blessing, both of them, each so different from the other, but each affectionate and loving to one who is their father. In this, I am most fortunate. I will set my mind to that.

Ch. 27

From Laura Place in Bath, September 1787

Dear Jane,

I write this in early morning before the house is a-stir in the hope that you are not languishing in the despair of widowhood. We must up and greet the morn with hope that this day will bring about renewed eagerness for what lies ahead. Here in Bath, not long from now we will begin the bustle of preparing for our morning stroll along the Avon and then to the Pump Room for our morning lounge. Oh, Jane, I cannot begin to describe the excitement I feel with each new sunrise. In only one week I have met and spoken with all sorts of people, men and women, young like myself and old like Mrs. Littleworth, who seems to know everybody. "Pass on by quickly," she will say about a perfectly presentable woman, dressed in high style, nothing about her person to suggest wrongdoing. "Pretend you do not notice her. It is rumoured that she has taken up with a bounder not her husband." I do as Mrs. Littleworth tells me, or at least I try my best. "Pick up your feet," she has whispered to me on more than one occasion. "You are shuffling." I do my best, not wishing to embarrass Mrs. Littleworth with my country ways.

However, my shuffling, as she calls it, comes not from the country but from the shoes I have been given to wear. In her haste to outfit me for proper society, Mrs. Littleworth neglected to order shoes for me. Thus, I am shuffling in shoes made for Mrs. Littleworth and much too large for me. I can only hope that the cobbler will make shoes to fit me, for on Tuesday next I will attend my first ball here. Most assuredly, I do not want to shuffle then.

I have had no word from Mr. Bennet. Mr. Littleworth has sent a note assuring his wife that the Bennet family is doing fine, that the children seem well and happy, though Mr. Bennet spends much time strolling about his fields, eyes on the ground, deaf to Mr. Littleworth's cheery greeting, kicking at stones and downed limbs. None of that surprises me. Mr. Bennet can play the part of wounded husband or sullen child ever so well; he has had much practice. And if I may be so bold, he might well spend some of his time not idling about the countryside but scratching out a note to his wife. He might admit in such a note that he looks forward to my return. As it is, I do not plan a return anytime soon, though of course I am but a guest here and beholden to Mrs. Littleworth. It is her bidding I must do, a welcome change from following Mr. Bennet's orders. Everything Mr. Bennet ordered I did not wish to do: reprimanding the servants, for instance, was difficult for me, having had no training in such duties. But I did my duty and, Mr. Bennet would have to agree—could he bring himself to do so—the household has run much more smoothly in recent weeks. And the children? He persisted in ordering me to, as he put it, "make them fit for civilized company." Piffle! I did not see that he was able to do that. Apparently the simple fact of their being at my breast—and not altogether successfully there, either—should have made me all-powerful, at least in the area of infant suasion. "Suasion" is a new word I learned in conversation with a gentleman one morning in the Assembly Rooms. "The suasion of young ladies is ever so preferable to force, don't you agree?" That's what he said whilst I struggled to imagine how it might be spelled so that Dr. Johnson's dictionary could enlighten me as to its meaning when I returned to Mrs. Littleworth's house. "Yes indeed," I answered. After all, just about anything is preferable to force; surely suasion would fall into that grouping. Each day my *vocabulary*—that refers to the words I know—grows. I find conversation much easier now than back at Longbourn. Could it be that the conversants I have met here have more conversation than the one I spend my time with in the country, that being Mr. Bennet? O Jane, I can hear you twisting your handkerchief. Rest assured that I remain a dutiful wife and mother.

But—and do not hate me for what I am about to confess—my greatest pleasure here in Bath is the freedom to do as I see fit. I am not chained to my children, bless their little souls, nor to household chores, nor to my husband's concupiscent demands. Are you surprised that your little sister is familiar with such a term as "concupiscent"? I only recently came upon it when, on a morning stroll along Green Park, I happened to hear one wag say to another, "But, dear fellow, concupiscence can be practiced with one's wife as well as with ladies of the evening." The other man seemed startled but then nodded rapidly up and down as if he had just opened a gift that pleased him. I sorted out in my mind the possible spelling of the word and on returning home flew to Dr. Johnson. There it was: "lust or strong desire." A thrill ran down my spine before I realized that of course such a word applied only to men. And then another thrill as I recalled the night of rapture with none other than Mr. Bennet. You can be sure that Mr. Bennet's concupiscence was much in evidence then. Fortunately, we women need not trouble ourselves, free as we are from concupiscence. We women are, because of such freedom, the stronger of the two sexes, and often, now that I am somewhat familiar with the word, I find myself pitying the men as they try, unsuccessfully, not to peer into the bosoms so artfully displayed by women here—and at every ball everywhere, I should think. Well, I shall be able to tell you more after Tuesday.

Should you so choose, you might drop a line to Mr. Bennet in which you enquire as to the well-being of the children. I will admit to missing them, though, truth be told, not very frequently. Do not think me an unfit mother, please. I accuse myself quite often enough.

And if you do drop him a line, you might hint that he does have a wife whose well-being seemingly holds no interest for him. I have received not so much as a note from him. For all he knows, I could be in dire distress or even dead. But then, he paid me small attention when I lived at Longbourn, where, in a manner of speaking I was as good as dead. So there.

As I seem to be in the mood for truth-telling, I confess to missing the early hours with Cook, planning for the day ahead. I much enjoyed sitting on the stool in her kitchen, popping crusts of warm sugar pie into my mouth as we conferred. Here, even though the kitchen is not made available to me, I cannot seem to shrink myself back into youthfulness. Each day I fear the disappearance of my waistline entirely come eventide.

Yr loving sister,
Marianne

Ch. 28

In Which I Despair

She has been gone a fortnight. Mr. Littleworth informs me that all is well in Bath. Would that this were so here at home. The children have become too much for Mrs. Rummidge. They are to be found throughout the house, in the pantry, the closet, beneath the dining table, under my bed! If I am not careful, I would trip over them, for they are everywhere, Elizabeth in the lead, Jane close behind. I shall take steps. But I shall not pen my thoughts to Mrs. Bennet. It is she who ought to do the penning. I shall do the acting, though what form that will take eludes me at the moment. I will admit to a certain uneasiness as to the whereabouts of Colonel Millar. He seems to me to be capable of a worrisome deviousness beneath all his grand manners. Perhaps I will ask Mr. Littleworth to pass the following on to Mrs. Bennet:

> "Thou shall not sow thy vineyard with diverse seeds, lest thou defile both."
>
> —Deuteronomy 22:9.

Perhaps I will deliver it myself.

Ch. 29

Dearest Jane,

My slippers are satin, their little heels named after Louis, a French person, who I am told wore them. The buckle is a beautiful silver so one could say that I will sparkle when I dance, which I will do this very evening at my very first dress ball to be held in the New Assembly Rooms. Mrs. Littleworth has secured two tickets from a Mr. Tyson since tickets are not available to ladies. Yet they are transferable to ladies. I do not think I will ever come to know the rules and regulations of this beautiful place, but I continue to try. Listening, I have found, is a very good way to learn. I have learned ever so many vocabulary words which I find make my conversation sparkle. At least, that's what I have been told during our morning walks when we are paused to pass the time of day with the gentlemen on parade. My slippers are a perfect fit, no shuffling at all.

According to Mrs. Littleworth, a new ladies' fashion is in evidence here. It, too, is from France whose queen is Marie Antoinette and who, according to rumour, may very well be out of favour, especially with the rabble who seem intent on turning things upside down in Paris. Heaven forfend. It is all very confusing. The Assembly Rooms are a-buzz with news from France, much of it to do with the perilous situation of the monarchy, something I cannot imagine happening here. I shall have to learn French. So much is to be learned of their culture. Occasionally, in conversation in one of the Assembly Rooms, a gentleman will begin to speak French, assuming that I of course will follow. That I cannot is an embarrassment to me; one gets the idea that people of quality are fluent in more than one language, the French language being the most popular at the moment. I have learned to say *mais oui*, which means "yes indeed." That seems to have sufficed so far. I'm not sure what *ma cherie* means, but I am determined to find out since so many of the gentlemen use that when they converse with me. I suspect it is a term of endearment. *Charmant*, I must say.

But I digress. The new fashion is called Empire, pronounced "Ahmpeer," just like the French country. It is quite different from what we are accustomed to and ever so much more comfortable. It is cut low, lower than we are used to, allowing for a surprising amount of bosom to show itself. Mother would have raised her eyebrows into her hair—as I can see you doing at this very moment. But it is the skirt that is the most different. It has no waist! My dear sister, can you imagine: the folds of the skirt are drawn up under the bosom where they are fastened with a brooch or a sweet flower and then allowed to flow, passing quite free of the waist and onto the tips of the slippers below. If I had known how to pray to heaven for something so gloriously perfect, I would have prayed for just such a gown. For, as I have reported to you in earlier letters, my waistline has all but disappeared. Just think: without this newest of costume I would have been required to wear a sash, and a very wide one at that, and no one would wish to escort such a pumpkin onto the ballroom floor, which, all praise to Marie Antoinette or Josephine or whoever, will not happen. Also, I need not cinch myself so tightly. I need not fear the bursting of seams or stays. *"Vive la France!"* That's French for "Hooray for France."

In keeping with the theme of Francais, I have discovered a novel—a French novel!—in Mrs. Littleworth's dressing room. She did not take it amiss that I should be in her private chambers; rather, she thrust the book at me and urged me to read it. It is entitled *Manon Lescaut*, which is French for the heroine's name. Fortunately, Mrs. Littleworth has seen to it that she has a copy written in English. I learn quickly, she tells me, but not that quickly. Perhaps I will be able to consume a few chapters this very afternoon before I begin my preparation for tonight's ball. I shall not chalk my face; the French have given that up for just a bit of rouge, which now that I see the word on the paper, looks

French. I shall enquire into its meaning from one of my dancing partners.

As you can see, I left Pamela back at Longbourn. She became quite dull once she was married, forever trying to get into high society when she wasn't even a lady and then she does thanks to her lord of a husband. This Manon, though, is French. I don't believe they look as favourably on marriage as we English.

Has Mr. Bennet written you news of Longbourn? I do not worry about the children since they are well cared for by Mrs. Rummidge. I do wonder, at times, about Mr. Bennet. Who is looking after him?

Yr loving sister,
Marianne

Ch. 30

O my dove, that art in the clefts of the rock,
in the secret places of the stairs, let me see thy countenance,
let me hear thy voice; for sweet is thy voice,
and thy countenance is comely.

—SONG OF SOLOMON 2:14

"Now, Tom," I said only a few days before this one, "your Mathilda's good efforts could bring you the additional income you are forever complaining to be in want of. We might even agree to your purchase of an acre of my property should you deem it right and proper that she settle into Longbourn, for the time being. Think, man!"

Tom did not seem to be in a thinking mood. He shook off the hand I had placed on his shoulder and said, "Begging your pardon, sir, but her mother is in need of Mathilda's efforts. The little ones need looking after; they are always underfoot, and they slow my wife's weaving almost to a stop. Mathilda scoops them up and amuses them with some game she has made up in her head. She keeps them neat and clean, for the most part, and she does the same for her mum and dad. I do not know what we would do without her." Tom looked glum.

"Exactly!" I answered him. "My daughters are becoming little ruffians. They scoot and crawl about beneath the furniture, under the feet of their nurse, if you could call her a nurse; they climb onto chairs and ladders. It is a wonder that one of them hasn't come to an untimely end. Oh, Tom"—I put my hand back on his shoulder—"it's the children we must think about, don't you agree?" And I added, "What with the extra guineas Mathilda would bring to you, your missus wouldn't need to keep up so much with her spinning and weaving and hauling cloth to market and all the other chores she does. She would be free to see to pleasing you. How long has it been since she's done that?"

Tom shook his head. "Too long, sir, too long indeed."

And so it is that Mathilda has come to live with us. Mrs. Rummidge is not at all pleased; indeed, she does not speak to me at all, a welcome relief since almost everything she has ever said to me was in the form of invective that I cannot bring myself to re-produce here. The other servants roll their eyes and dart in the other direction when they see me. I should think they would be relieved as well not to have my children underfoot. But then, one never knows about servants; they are the most secretive of breeds.

As for the children themselves, they seem happy and content. Jane, who is struggling to enter the world of language, says, when I point to Mathilda, "Mama!" Everyone laughs then, save for Elizabeth, who shakes her head so vigorously that her red curls toss about like sparks from a wildfire.

As for myself, I am most relieved to be free of the worry that my children are not being cared for properly. Mathilda, as hearty and as healthy as my ewes down in the pasture, brings her good spirits and willing hands to our household. She seems happy to be away from the chores down in her mother's home and in her father's field. Here she can for a short time imagine herself mistress of Longbourn. Until Mrs. Bennet returns, of course. Assuming she does.

I have yet to exchange my mourning suits for the coats and breeches of winter. I find myself wondering whether Mrs. Bennet, mother of my late infant son, finds her mourning garb oppressive and if so, what she will exchange it for. Something in keeping with her role as wife and mother, I hope.

I have yet to determine whether or not to apprise Mrs. Bennet of this recent addition to our household. Mr. Littleworth will no doubt have an opinion. I shall seek it anon. On the other hand, perhaps not.

Ch. 31

Dear Sister,

I trust that you are well. Colonel Millar appeared at the ball. We shall walk together this very afternoon in Sydney Gardens. Forgive me, I am in a tizzy.

I know, dear sister, that what I tell you suggests that I have not heeded your advice. I know that from the very beginning of my journey you have in your letters warned me of the seductiveness of such brilliance as is to be found in this most fashionable city. You have cautioned me against the dissembling you assured me awaited me here. "False promises are everywhere," you wrote, "not least in the glittering society of the idle class. Mind that you do not fall prey to one of those dandies whose chief aim is to make you his plaything." Such has not happened, dear sister, I swear! *Rien!* as the French would say. Or they might say, *rien de tout*, which means "nothing at all." You see how accomplished I am becoming. And I am reading daily from Mrs. Littleworth's not inconsiderable library. However, I do not recommend that you read the French novel *Manon Lescaut*, for it would serve only to heighten your worries over life in Society. Which is where I am at this moment. I am in Society. And I am in it with Colonel Millar.

Long ago, it now seems to me, in a letter to you I opined that women were not subject to the passions that men seemed incapable of curbing; in that, I pronounced us the superior sex. How foolish of me! Because now, I am consumed by wave after wave of passion when in the company of Colonel Millar. Which is as often as I can manage it. I place myself on paths where I know he walks and in rooms where I know he comes to discuss the matters of the day. I am as close to throwing myself at his feet as my shred of propriety will allow. And I am without shame, for it is he that causes my knees to weaken and my heart to beat so that I fear he must hear it. It is he that brings the flush to my cheeks and causes my eyes to shine. It is he whose absence I cannot bear. And I have been successful in my pursuit, for he has been my almost constant companion during my time in Bath. He makes me happy. He is my colonel and I am his. And yes, I have not forgotten that I am a wife and a mother and the mistress of Longbourn, and yet all of those responsibilities recede with each passing hour I spend with the colonel. It is as if I were being steered by an invisible hand; I seem to have lost control of the girl who lived at Longbourn, and in her stead there has risen a passionate woman, for whom life unfolds in all its brilliance. I am becoming a true woman.

Allow me to explain how all this came to pass: First, let me assure you that Mrs. Littleworth has been at my side during the whole of this visit. She has provided advice and counsel and, I will admit, protection from those who flirt mercilessly in the hope of securing a new plaything, as you call it. But she has come to take the waters for her rheumatism and a rapid heart beat, and so today she has left me to my own devices while she immerses herself in the healing pools of the hot springs. I do hope she finds some relief from the discomfort that bedevils her every step. She shows great courage in insisting on accompanying me on our morning strolls. In the Assembly Rooms she passes the time mainly in the card room, though I know her fingers are too stiff to make the game a pleasant one. Nonetheless, she goes about the duties of Society insofar as they will serve to make me accepted and admired. Her generosity shows itself in every gown, every slipper, every jewel I wear. She sees that tradesmen and dressmakers and shoemakers and milliners are paid directly and fairly without argument, without bargaining, without discussion. I cannot imagine Mr. Bennet's reaction were he to be presented with a bill for such elegance; I am most fortunate to have Mrs. Littleworth as a most devoted friend for whom money means little more than what it can buy, in this case my adornment.

I confess that I have kept to myself today's plan to

walk in the gardens with Colonel Millar. I am quite certain that, were Mrs. Littleworth to know, she would forbid it despite her pronouncement that she wishes only happiness for me. But then I have also heard it said, "What one doesn't know, can't hurt one." Have you heard that, dear Jane? The colonel whispered it in my ear as we sipped punch at the ball.

The ball: I shall remember it all the days of my life. Or rather I shall remember dancing with the colonel resplendent in his red coat and black, shining boots. The rest of the ball remains a blur. "May I have the pleasure, mademoiselle?" he said. Clearly, he believed I was in Society, for he used the French term of address, which means, in English, "miss." I did not advise him that he was speaking to a "madame." Do not chide me, sister. I have much to tell.

It was a minuet so I was much at ease, having danced just about every kind of minuet anyone could ever have imagined right there in Meryton when I was but a girl. Thus, I was free to make conversation, which I did and, out of nervousness, quite rapidly, too. I cannot recall at this moment about what: about the minuet, I would guess, or the musical accompaniment, which is made much more musical here by the presence of violin, cello, a guitar, and a flute. I must have gone on at some length, I suppose, for the colonel interrupted me to say, "Do you talk as a rule while you are dancing?"

"I am quite impressed by the size of this room, are you not?" I answered.

"I am impressed by some of the people within this room." He smiled down at me and continued, "By one person in this room in particular."

"And who," I asked in the archest manner possible, "might that be?"

"I believe you know who that person is," he answered.

I tossed my curls a bit. "No, who?" I asked.

"My partner in dance," he said, "as you are well able to guess. It gives me great delight to know that this particular minuet lasts a good half an hour. I do not believe I should ever tire of seeing your curls dance about your lovely shoulders. I would that the dance might continue forever."

Now, Jane, what should I have said in answer to that? I must have blushed, for I felt the blood rush to my cheeks. "You are too kind, sir." And then, Jane, I thought to strike while the iron was hot. I summoned all my courage and said, "Could we have met somewhere before this?" Without waiting for his answer, I rushed ahead. "Perhaps it is your uniform, for in my childhood village of Meryton I encountered many dressed as you, though of course not so elegantly." I smiled up at him. He was of great height, Jane, though not so tall that I could not feel the brush of his lips on my temple when the minuet brought us close.

"Surely I would have remembered," he returned, "if that girl was you."

I wanted to scream, But it was! It was I whom you danced with. It was I you held in your arms and kissed into breathlessness and led so sweetly beneath the elms and O my dear colonel, it was you who gave me your greatest gift. Her name is Jane and she is the loveliest of all children and she looks much like you, with your deep blue eyes and your gentle disposition. O my dear colonel, claim your right to your daughter and to the woman you hold in your arms at this very moment. We are yours. Take us with you. Wherever you lead, there shall we follow. But I said none of this. For once I held my tongue; for once common sense overcame the rush of emotion that threatened to topple everything I knew.

"May I be so bold," he said, "as to enquire if you will come out with me on the morrow? I must see you again."

"Yes," I murmured. And the dance ended. We danced twice again during the evening. Mrs. Littleworth took no notice, busy as she was at the card table. I took no notice of anyone but him. As far as I was concerned, we were the only couple at the ball.

"Let us keep our plans to ourselves," he whispered. "What one doesn't know can't hurt one."

So yes, in just a few hours we shall commence our stroll in Sydney Gardens where I understand one can get lost in the mazes should one lose one's head.

Do not fear for me, sister. My future is safe with him.

What is this I hear from Longbourn? Mr. Bennet has

taken a new servant? Mathilda, she of the farm? Good grief! Mrs. Rummidge scratched out a note delivered to me here. I did not think that she could write, poor thing, and from what I see before me, I am not far wrong.

I know you wish me safe. Wish me well, too.

Yrs affectionately,
Marianne

Ch. 32

'Tis better to bear the ills we have
than fly to others that we know not of.

—WILLIAM SHAKESPEARE

That damned Millar! He paid no heed to the order of the village judge that he and his hell-bound friends ride clear of my property. Indeed, out of necessity Tom enclosed the property so that Millar would know full well where his land ended and mine began. But no, he, or his hunting acquaintances and their mounts, simply tore down the fence in some places and in others jumped over the fence, crying Tally-ho or some such rubbish. I shall certainly speak to the colonel when next I see him. In the meantime, I have spent many daylight hours repairing the damage. Tom, of course, has given me his able hand e'en though enclosure of land, any land, is not to his liking. A good man, Tom.

Tom's Mathilda, while not as strong as her father, is fleet of foot. She has taken to running in the direction opposite of myself. Surely she knows I mean her no harm; however, something must have happened to turn her from me. It cannot be that little kiss I planted on her plump and juicy lips just as she was coming from the pantry, her apron tight over her ample bosom, smudges of flour dotting her glorious curls. She looked good enough to eat and so I allowed myself a tiny taste, no harm meant, no harm done. However, things between us have not been cordial since then. I see more of her back than I do of her bosom. And so I have been forced to hide myself around corners of the hallways and leap out when she approaches. Damned if she doesn't almost jump out of her skin, a sight I wouldn't mind seeing, truth be told. "Oh, sir!" she cries. "You gave me such a start!" Then off she goes. It would not become me to run after her, but little surprises here and there could not offend, and who knows but that I will catch her. A surprise for both of us then!

This past week she has found her way into all of my reveries. Silly game, this. Not unlike those blasted hunters chasing after their doomed foxes, ruining fences and property not theirs. Mathilda, though, is my property, at least for the time being, but since I intend no execution of any plan, she is safe from marauding sportsmen. I shall see to that.

No word from Bath. Mr. Littleworth assures me all is well. I would rather Mrs. Bennet assured me herself. I wish she would pen me a note. Why she does not is quite beyond me. Perhaps tomorrow.

She is good with the children—Mathilda, that is. Jane of course is happy with everyone; Elizabeth, who is happy with no one save Mrs. Rummidge, seems to have taken quite readily to Mathilda. The three of them spend long afternoons in the sunshine down in the meadow farthest from the house. Perhaps one day I shall surprise them there.

Ch. 33

Dear Jane,

I am filled with shame and yet I am not. Are you sitting down? I allowed Colonel Millar to take liberties with my person. It all seemed so innocent. For a few afternoons we walked about the parks and along the river, talking as we went. He seemed to enjoy my Frenchifying, though I was careful not to over-do it lest I seem to be putting on airs. By the way, *ma cherie* means "my dear." That's what the colonel began to call me. *Ma cherie*. O la! The sound of a man who speaks French! It comes from deep within his throat and travels upward until it spills like honey into my ears and I am made deaf to common sense.

But let me tell you all: I pray that you will not harden your heart against me, for now as in no other moment of my life I need your kind understanding. Mrs. Littleworth has found considerable relief from the waters and so she has spent every afternoon and early evening in their presence. I, therefore, have been left unchaperoned. I did not concern myself with her absence; after all, I am a grown woman and can properly look after myself. The colonel, however, did take note and began his campaign.

At first we talked of Longbourn and Northfield and of the Littleworths. We laughed over my memory of Mr. Littleworth always hungry, always waiting for his dinner like a dog who has been kept away from his dish for too long and is starving. I agree, Jane, this picture does not seem all that amusing now that I write it, but at the time I, in my giddiness, thought it hilarious. I could not stop laughing. I am not laughing now.

The colonel and I did not talk of Mr. Bennet nor of my children. We did not speak of my marriage vows or of his military assignments. We did not speak of his sister. And finally, on the night in question, we did not speak at all.

It was, for autumn, a balmy evening. We had been to the theatre, a lovely little play about magic potions and queens falling in love with donkeys, in the forest, so delightful, so silly. I wore yet another dress Mrs. Littleworth had ordered made for me, this one a creamy white *peau de soie*, translation to come later, neckline modestly low, enhanced by much tulle, and sashed in an azure silk. My bonnet, too, was swathed in tulle to complement my dress and to frame my face as if I were a beautiful painting. The colonel presented me with a sweet bouquet of violets—in September no less!—and I fastened it beneath my breasts just there in the center. No need for my pelisse, no need for anything except the strong presence of this man, his hand firm beneath my elbow, my arms bare of gloves, of sleeve, of all but his touch.

As we walked from the theatre, he suggested a carriage ride around Sydney Gardens. I agreed and shortly we found ourselves close together, the driver of the carriage a very old man not at all curious about his fares. "I do remember you, *ma cherie*," the colonel said. "A village girl, as I recall, light and pleasant in my arms." I nodded. He said, "And now you are grown into a woman, a beautiful woman. I count myself fortunate to have found you again." He took his cloak from his shoulders and placed it over mine. He leaned into me as he did, tipped my chin up with his hand ever so gently, and kissed me full on the mouth. "Forgive me," he said. "I find you impossible to resist."

"And I you," I answered and raised my mouth up for another kiss. And another. Even now, after everything, Be still my heart.

As I look back, perched as I am on the ledge of despair, I know I should have chanced breaking the spell. I should have reminded him of our brief meeting at the festival, he with his sister, I with my husband and children. Perhaps then, the suffering that awaited me would never have occurred or would not have been so painful. But no, such common sense had no chance. I was as a girl blossoming into womanhood before his very eyes. Foolish, oh, how foolish.

The following evening we strolled in the garden in the maze, in the labyrinth; I scarcely knew where I was going, only that I would follow him wherever he led. On the third evening, as we walked, he drew me into an alcove, kissed me, and said, "Come away with me. I am called to Devon on Monday next. We shall be together there." With that, he cupped my breast with his hand and kissed me there where I was the softest, where the scent of his violets rose to fill the air. I was as close to a genuine swoon as ever I have been. "Yes," I breathed.

I slept not a wink that night. I tossed and turned until almost morning, longing for him, afraid of our future together, afraid for my future without him, fearful of Mrs. Littleworth's low opinion of me, and regretful for what I could no longer be for Mr. Bennet. And here I must confess that even in the most intimate moments with Mr. Bennet my thoughts flew not to my husband but to my colonel. Alas.

Dawn crept through my window at last, and I knew what I would do. I would do as he asked. I would need only the time to return to Longbourn and claim the colonel's rightful child. I did not care that I would be branded a harlot or, worse, a negligent mother or, worse, a divorced woman should I become one. It was not a new marriage that I wanted; my old one is quite enough. What I wanted was to lose myself in him, to feel the rush of passion at his touch that burned like fire and soothed like gentle waters, his lips soft yet insistent on mine. I wanted all this not just for this hour but forever. Thus, I believed, I would become the woman I was meant to be.

I imagined that the three of us would live as one in a village by the sea. Or, should he so desire, we would reside at Northfield. I would be proud to be mistress of such a grand estate, though, in a rare burst of practicality, I believed that settling some distance from Longbourn would be in the best interest of us all. As for Mr. Bennet, he would recover quickly, and as for Elizabeth, she is happiest when I am not with her. Mrs. Rummidge or that Mathilda my husband has hired would see to her needs, most of which she seems prepared to meet herself. Willful child, Elizabeth.

I wish that I had not read *Manon Lescaut* all the way through. Manon and her lover flee, too, to Louisiana of all places—where is that!—and she catches a cold in the swamp and dies. Oh dear. Well, 'tis but a story and French at that. *Quelle* unrealistic.

Tomorrow we will dine and plan our future. I cannot wait. I must be with him. He is my life.

Ch. 34

In Which I Bring About My Own Disgrace

It is my decision that this diary be prohibited to anyone save my own eyes. I do not wish my heirs or curious strangers niggling their way into my private shame. However, I will continue to keep the diary, as I have found it quite a necessary companion to me who recently has found himself in unusual and embarrassing straits. Still, I do not wish my heirs to see me as womanish inasmuch as tears have fallen, and so I will confine my thoughts to this diary and this diary only and on my death I order whoever finds it to burn it to the ground next to where I will lie, untended, unmourned, unheralded. No less than I deserve.

Thusly do I confess. Mathilda proceeded to drive me

wild with desire. She fled from me whenever I drew near. She armed herself with my children, which is to say she perched Jane on one hip, Elizabeth on the other, and strode the hallways and the drawing room like a ship with both guns blazing from her gunwales. I was defeated before I declared war. Which eventually I did. This estate belongs to me, as does everything within it, including this young strumpet. How dare she provoke me into lustful thoughts with her plump shoulders, her trim ankles, her flourishing bosom, her tiny waist, her nipples rising against the roughness of her apron, the . . . I decided to assert my authority. I would conquer her with a full frontal assault aided by my faithful servant, the ever-ready Mrs. Rummidge. It would serve Mrs. Bennet right for refusing my pleas for congress; it would release me from the torment of unfulfilled desire; it would set things right.

Now, I was perfectly aware that the involvement of a servant, especially one so impertinent as Mrs. R., might not be wise. But how, otherwise, would I be able to persuade so young and untried a lass as Mathilda to take her place in a bed alongside me, her employer, for heaven's sake, whom, I must admit, she could very well fear. Hence, my plan, born of delusion and desire, was hatched: On a dark night Mrs. Rummidge would appear to take sick. From her bed she would call for help. Mathilda would come running. "Oh, Mathilda," Mrs. Rummidge would say, "I have caught a chill. I am so cold and cannot make myself warm. Please comfort me by laying yourself down next to me, you who are so warm and so full of animal spirits." Mathilda would of course comply. Once abed, she would discover that Mrs. Rummidge was not alone, that I, her master, lay on just the other side of Mrs. Rummidge. At this point, Mrs. Rummidge would leap from the bed, leaving only the two of us—Mathilda and yours truly—to clasp each other till all passion was spent.

Will it surprise you when I tell you that the plan failed? That it never even got to the battlefield? It will certainly not surprise you when I tell you that my aide-de-camp, Mrs. Rummidge, deserted her superior officer, but not before upbraiding him mercilessly.

"You should be ashamed of yourself," she said when I approached her with my plan. "You are a husband to my little one, my Marianne. God help her—God help you—if you do this dastardly deed!" And here she shook her crooked finger directly into my face.

"Mrs. Rummidge," I countered, "may I remind you of your place here? I am master, you are my servant. You are to do as I ask."

"Servants knows rights and wrongs, sir. And what you are up to is not right. Not for young Mathilda, either. Think of her." She grew red in her face again.

"I am thinking of her," I said. "I think of her all the time. I am asking you for your help. No, I am demanding it."

"You shall not have it. Furthermore, I will remove your children from this house and place them into the safety of my house in the village."

I doubt that Mrs. Rummidge has a house in the village. She is so full of lies that I had believed that this one little lie I was asking her to participate in would be in keeping with her prevaricating self, that she might take pleasure from the little trick I had proposed. "You will not kidnap my children," I said firmly.

"Then give up this plan for deceit and ravagement."

"I have no plan for ravagement, as you call it. Whatever happens will be by mutual consent. And now, if you please, return to your duties, whatever they are." This did not seem the time to ascertain exactly what her duties were or whether she did in fact have a home in the village. It was time for me to re-assert our proper places in the infinite scheme of things. "Should your duties not be to your liking, you are free to return to that village of yours."

She turned to leave the room, then paused to point her finger once again in the direction of my nose: "My duty is to your poor dear wife. She is yet but a child. She is often lonely and afraid. She is my lost lamb, and I will use any means to protect her until she can discover how to protect herself." And she fled, though not before she called out, "I will leave when my little one insists. And not before." She was gone. Good lord, how that woman talks.

But I was through with such talk. I had had enough of

peering through keyholes and hiding behind draperies and putting myself in Mathilda's path in the miserable hope that at some point she would yield of her own accord. It is a truth universally acknowledged that if you want something done right, you had best do it yourself. And so I did. And lived to regret it.

That very night, after Mrs. Rummidge's excoriation of my plan, I made sure that all in the house was quiet. I tiptoed quietly up the steep stairway that I knew led to Mathilda's room. I paused on the landing to make sure no one was about and that the girl was in her room. Thusly, I proceeded. I was most careful not to burst in, for I knew that she might scream or at least be somewhat startled and cry out. I turned the knob of the door very quietly and very quietly let myself into the room. She lay in her bed, eyes closed, and I crossed to her bed and, bending down, I whispered, "Be not afraid. I am come to satisfy you." In an instant she leapt from her bed and made for the door. I blocked the way. "You ought be filled with joy, my girl," I said, "and so leave off your protests. Believe me, I will not hurt you."

She stood upright, stock-still, her nightdress a bit torn at the breast, and pleaded. "Oh, sir," she said, "please do not take my virtue from me. I have naught but that. I am poor and unschooled, but I am pure. It is all that I have to offer a man who might one day make me his wife." She clutched at her nightdress, her hair tumbling over her shoulders, her dark eyes bright with fear, and I felt the lust rise in me again. I advanced. She stumbled and fell onto the bed, all fight gone from her. Tears flowed from her eyes and streamed down her cheeks. "Oh please, sir, I beg of you."

Was I to bow to her pleas and scurry away like some rodent? Was I not a man and a man of property at that? Was I not born with certain rights and privileges? Was I not ignored and even shunned and, from the look of things, abandoned by my own wife? Was it not true that I lived in a house without warmth, without company, without affection? Should I not have what I deserved? After all, she was but a mere servant, and so yes, I would have my way with her, no matter that she was but a girl, although one who had served me well, a girl who had comforted and amused my children, who had brought nothing but happiness into this house.

Perhaps it was that, the sweet purity of her nature to which, lord knows, I was so unaccustomed that prevented my advance, for suddenly a blast of cold air—reason, perhaps?—swept across my forehead, dashing the film from my eyes and rooting me where I stood. For the first time in many months I saw truth: the girl lying helpless on her servant's bed was not Mathilda but my wife in the marriage bed weeping uncontrollably and utterly miserable over what lay ahead. In that moment I saw myself as my wife and how this poor girl Mathilda must see me: a beast bent on making his kill. Desire fled; shame took its place. "Forgive me," I said and turned to leave. "Forgive me," I repeated, remorse rising in me as desire had risen only moments before.

Then I heard it. "Papa!" I had neglected to close the door to the hallway and there on the threshold stood Jane and Elizabeth. How long they had been there I could not know, but it was long enough to frighten them. Tears ran down Jane's cheeks. Elizabeth, too, was moved, but to anger. "No, no!" she cried and tottered toward the bed. I had by this time restored my person to respectability and I knelt down to take my children in my arms. Finally, after what seemed an eternity Jane ceased her sobbing, Elizabeth left off striking my back with her little fists. The three of us knelt together clinging to each other and to any shred of decency that my lecherousness had not devoured. Behind us, Mathilda lay exhausted, her virtue intact.

How could I have behaved in so dastardly a fashion? How could I have allowed my animal nature to overwhelm my good and noble self? I had not debased Mathilda; I had debased myself, and in the eyes of my children I was no more than a mad creature of the wild, a thing to run from. And what had I done to my wife? Our life together, as I had imagined it, collapsed before my very eyes. No wonder she had flown to Bath. Safety was there, not here.

I do not know at this writing if my children have forgiven me. I surely asked it of them, of Mathilda as well. But it remains quiet here in this house, as if everyone has gone out, as if everyone has moved away, as if everyone is in hiding. As surely they would should a monster such as I be allowed to roam at large.

I must do better.

From Longbourn, October of '87

My dear wife,

I write to enquire when you might be returning to us here at home. We are well, but your absence is felt by all, and we wish for your speedy return. You will scarcely recognize your little girls, they have grown so and are speaking quite coherently now. You will note on your return that we are absent one of the staff: Mathilda has returned to the farm where her mother finds herself in need of her. Otherwise, all is as you left it, including Mrs. Rummidge.

As for myself I am somewhat at a loss without your good direction and pleasing ways; I have given serious thought to visiting you in Bath, though not without an invitation from you. Until such is forthcoming, may I say that nothing will please me more than to see you running up the steps to Longbourn once more ne'er to roam again, at least not so far and not for so long.

Mr. Littleworth, also surprised by his wife's long absence, gives me to understand that you are becoming fluent in the French language. Therefore, I shall bid you adieu, ma cherie.

Your loving husband,
Edward

Ch. 35

Dear Jane,

I am distraught, humiliated, embarrassed to death, and by none other than Mr. Bennet, who promised to wait for my invitation but who nevertheless showed himself most unexpectedly and most inappropriately just as the colonel and I had arranged ourselves in a quiet corner of the bistro's terrace. The leaves in the nearby trees overlooking the *jardin* (garden) sighed, a few dropping at our feet; the sweet zephyrs of fall wafted o'er us and the perfume of nearby autumn grasses made my head swim in a very pleasant way. 'Tis true, 'tis autumn, but here in Bath it is a gentle season with only an occasional shiver rising against the coming winter. I had just shivered; the colonel was about to place my lovely muslin shawl about my shoulders when who should appear but my husband of all people, looking much the worse for wear, clumsy as only he can be, tripping his way onto the terrace and almost falling into the bistro before he righted himself. Fortunately, this being late in the season, past-season actually, the place was deserted except for we three.

We three: now, there's a phrase. I shrieked from surprise while at the same time I could not help but notice the contrast in the appearances of the two men: the colonel so elegant in his frock coat of silk, his white linen shirt so crisp, his hair drawn back from his forehead and tied back at the nape of his dear neck, so modest yet so refined. Mr. Bennet, on the other hand—now, granted he had come some distance and clearly had not taken an opportunity to refresh himself or his travel clothes—looked more countrified than ever: his woolen stockings, one of them slumped toward his shoe; his breeches askew, as was his hair, thinner than when I last saw it. He breathed heavily, his face grew redder, and I feared for what would come next. Briefly, I thought to reach out and dust him off, to straighten his waistcoat, to pull up his stocking. Indeed, my heart went out to him so awkward and out of place he was. But I restrained myself; I chose to remain silent, yet another poor choice, one among many, as I came to discover.

The colonel spoke first, no doubt because Mr. Bennet, out of breath as he was, could not. "My dear man," he said, "do recover yourself. Pray, be seated." He held out a chair. Mr. Bennet landed himself in it. "You seem to have exerted yourself inordinately." Mr. Bennet looked as if he would speak but couldn't, his mouth ajar most unattractively. The colonel stood, looking down on him, and said, "Your delightful wife has given me the pleasure of her company on this lovely afternoon." Mr. Bennet began to sputter. "In your absence," the colonel continued, "I saw it as my duty to relieve her loneliness and introduce her to some of the delights of Bath." He moved the toe of his beautifully appointed shoe about the flagstone of the terrace; it was as if he were dancing. Be still, my heart.

I must have smiled at the sight because Mr. Bennet's face began to redden once more. This time, however, he found words. "You bounder, Millar! You have lured my wife to this ungodly place so as to have your way with her!"

The colonel gasped. "Heaven forfend, sir, that I should have improper designs on your—"

I attempted to intervene at this point, certain that I had every right to do so. "Mr. Bennet," I began, but before I could continue, Mr. Bennet spoke in a voice so loud I was grateful for there being no other patrons.

"And about my property," he sputtered. "Do not think for one moment that you can get away with it."

"Get away with what?" Clearly the colonel was as confused as I by all this fuss.

"You know what I mean, sir. I refer to your hounds and your horses running rampant over my land. But all this is for another time. At present I am concerned with your running rampant over my wife!" The colonel smiled at this.

Mr. Bennet did not. I was silent, since neither of them appeared to remember that this fracas revolved around *moi* and both continued to ignore me. Suddenly Mr. Bennet seized my arm and drew me up from where I sat. "Right now, I shall escort my wife to her lodgings, where she will remain safe from the salacious attentions of one who purports to be the soul of honour but who in fact is a cad and a blackguard." He looked at me, finally, and said, "Do not shriek." I had no choice but to obey.

The colonel, cool and composed still, said, "I should call you out, Bennet, for impugning my good name and reputation."

"Then do so," said Mr. Bennet, "for you are no gentleman."

It was then that, despite my husband's directive, I screamed and, in between screams, promised to go on screaming until threats of a duel were disappeared. "I will not have it, I won't!" And I stamped my foot.

Allow me to pause here, dear sister, to offer an observation, though not one that came at the moment but upon later reflection. It is this: When men speak to each other cordially or angrily, in simple conversation or heatedly in passion, they ignore any woman near or far. It is as if we were mere pieces of fluff that they would brush off their coat collars. What is it that draws men together? Perhaps it is that they are relieved finally to have met an equal, no woman being up to that. Perhaps it is that at last they have met an adversary worthy of their attention. Perhaps it is that they enjoy combat without the likelihood of a shriek or a faint. So is it any wonder that we women must often make a scene such as I was making at this very moment? Oh, the racket we are capable of! A point of pride, I must say; a small one, but still.

However, so as to forestall another outburst, the colonel bowed and said, "As you wish, dear lady."

My husband hauled me down the path. He can be quite strong when he wishes. I did not, however, have to be silent. "Who is the gentleman here, Mr. Bennet?" I hissed. I wrenched my way out of his grasp. "Not you, I can assure you." And I turned to flee with the colonel. But he was not there. Alas, I had no choice but to follow my husband, pitiful creature he looked standing alone in the middle of the path.

Late That Night, at Mrs. Littleworth's

I am exhausted, but I must finish this letter so that it will reach you as quickly as possible.

As you might imagine, dear Jane, there was a scene. I thought I might fare better if I took the offensive, although, first, I must assure you that in no way could it be even imagined, except by Mr. Bennet, of course, that I was in the wrong. I am assuming that Mr. B., bumpkin that he is, is not accustomed to the ways of a more sophisticated society such as resides in Bath. Here flirtation is the rule of the day. Indeed, if one has youth and a bit of charm on her side, one is expected to flirt, and after a few wrong turns, I flirted delightfully, so I was told. Yes, admittedly, Mr. B. did find me with the colonel, whose attentions appear, granted, a bit more than flirtatious. But I remain the proper woman I have always been whilst sojourning in Bath, despite the suspicions of my husband. And yet I must confess to you, dear sister, that remaining that proper woman is not part of my plan, which has not changed in its tiniest detail: I shall endeavour to meet with my colonel until such time as I can reveal the truth, that little Jane is his. After that, I expect that the three of us will make haste to a destination where pettiness such as that demonstrated by Mr. Bennet does not exist. London seems a likely destination. But I get ahead of myself. First, the scene:

"How did you know where to find me?" I demanded once he'd hurried me into Mrs. Littleworth's rooms. Quickly I changed from my afternoon gown into an even more flattering dressing gown whose drapes and folds hid my burgeoning lower self, at the same time outlining my hips and breasts. O Jane, I know, I am impossible, but in the absence of a sword or musket, what weapon do we women have but our looks—and our wits? I chide myself, though not as quickly as you have already done.

"Mr. Littleworth provided me with that information. And so I came here to your lodgings thinking to find you in a mood to consider returning to Longbourn. I waited and waited and at last left these rooms and ventured out in hopes of discovering a bookshop."

Yes, of course, he would find for himself a bookshop. Somewhere to hide himself. "And were you successful? With the bookshop, I mean?" Perhaps I could distract him from the scolding I knew was at hand. So tiresome.

"Yes, indeed, I was pleased to discover an elegant volume of Montaigne's essays; fits right here in my breast pocket." He tapped his lapel.

"Fortunate. A perfect resting place. And so your visit to Bath has rewarded you."

"Indeed it has, in a way. In another, not at all. For, upon emerging from the shop, I was almost cut down by a carriage hell-bent on a destination unknown to me. Imagine my surprise when I saw that the carriage held persons familiar to me: you and Colonel Millar."

"Ah yes, the carriage." I could not think of anything reasonable enough to explain my presence in that carriage.

"The two of you looked to be quite the intimates. I could not keep my anger to myself. I determined to find you out. And so I did. And discovered you in what anyone would see as a compromising position there in that bistro, or whatever fashionable people call it. Will you offer an explanation? Is there an explanation?"

Hoping to distract him once more, since clearly my dressing gown was not performing as I had hoped, I said,

"And Mr. Littleworth, how is his health? He seemed quite apoplectic when he dined with us."

"How is Mr. Littleworth? He is surprised, that's how he is, surprised that his wife has remained in Bath since he cut off her funds some time ago."

"Why, the old skinflint! Why would he do that?"

"He mumbled something about her gambling debts, said she spent too much time at the tables."

"Not so! She takes the waters daily and in the evening calls on friends."

"Since you are rarely at home in the evenings, or so I assume, you cannot be certain that the friends she calls on do not reside in the gambling halls."

"If her funds have been cut off, what pleasure would the tables have for her? And incidentally, I have seen no dropping off of services here at her home, nor ever a mean table, and she has been most generous with my wardrobe. Are you certain that Mr. Littleworth remembered correctly? He is, as you very well know, somewhat aged."

"He was most definite. 'For the last time,' he said when he reported his wife's excesses to me. So my dear, if life here remains unchanged, the money must come from a source not her husband."

"This is all very tiresome," I answered, and shivered so that the gown slipped from my shoulder. I have found that shivering as an artifice can be most rewarding. Not so this time, alas.

"It is tiresome and so I will bring it to an end. You are returning to Longbourn with me. At once." And he added, frowning and growling, "If I have to drag you."

At this point he rose from the settee where he had been wringing his hands and gnashing his teeth in my direction and moved as if to do exactly what he proposed. Just as he reached for me, who should enter the room but Mrs. Littleworth! An angel in disguise.

"I could not help but hear the two of you," she said. "Like children, I must say, and as a grown woman of long experience, I must say that you, Mr. Bennet, will not take this girl from this house against her will." My goodness, she seemed to increase in size with every breath and almost to tower over Mr. Bennet, who continued with his bluster though he remained unheeded by anyone. "She is welcome here for as long as she wishes to be here, and if you continue to behave like a pirate, I shall summon the law. We shall see then who's in the right. And, I might add, we shall see what happens when this tawdry tale makes its way back to Longbourn. You could very well find yourself the laughing stock of the entire county." She moved toward the bell rope and added, "And for your information, Mr. Littleworth's threat to render me penniless is of little interest to me. You see, good fortune has been with me at the tables—in fact, very good." Mr. Bennet collapsed back onto the settee.

Why does he seat himself that way? He slumps and his knees go akimbo and the buttons on his waistcoat look as if they will pop and his linen shows. Only in his library have I seen him seated in an upright and attentive position, looking almost elegant, I must say. But here, on Mrs. Littleworth's most fashionable settee, he looked so beaten down, so forlorn, so just plain tired that again I could not help but feel a bit of sympathy for him—not enough to accompany him back to Longbourn, of course, but a genuine *frisson* (little shiver) nonetheless. "Thank you, Mrs. Littleworth," I said. "I have no intention of accompanying Mr. Bennet back to Longbourn at this time, certainly not under these circumstances. Manhandling is not to my taste now, nor was it ever." With that, I swept my robe back onto my shoulder and left the room.

Now what, dear Jane? I must somehow inform the colonel that I remain here of my own free person and am eager to resume our *rendezvous* (little meeting). My, my, soon you will know French as well as I. Until then, I shall enquire of Mrs. Littleworth what next I must do. She will, I am sure, be understanding and wise as she has in all things á la Bath. At least, and to my relief, Mr. Bennet has gone. Where I do not care.

Votre soeur,
Marianne

Ch. 36

Quaenam ista jocandi Saevitia!

"With a sporting cruelty!"

—CLAUDIAN

I am back to searching Montaigne, my only companion, for some understanding of or at least some comfort from the anguish laid upon me by my wife's "sporting cruelty." For the first time I see myself as she sees me: a boorish, awkward country lout without the wit or the strength or the wisdom to return her to her rightful home. I have always been thus, I suppose, but if one is to speak the truth—as one is obligated to in these pages—better a lout than a tart. That is what she seemed to me: dressed in all that finery, colour on her face and lips, and playing the part of a tease. Unforgivable! I shall not even go into her behaviour: eyebrows up and down, licking of lips, darting of tongue, sashaying this way and that, and in a dressing gown that is intended only for the darkest of night! Such a gown is worn surely for display, for tantalizing, for tarting! There, I've said it again.

Nothing I saw of her behaviour or appearance was in the least like the Marianne I brought to Longbourn only a few short years ago. Except for the screaming, which has always accompanied her, she was a stranger to me. And yet, there remains something about her that makes me want to protect her—from herself, it would seem—and take her away from the pretentiousness and the falseness that is Bath. Granted, I saw very little of the place. But I saw enough to know that no one who is my wife will enjoy its seductions for very long without suffering a terrible aftermath.

I am aware that I have avoided the topic of Colonel Millar. The thought of him and Marianne so close together in that café makes for too much pain. The memory of the way my wife looked at him, as she had never looked at me, will remain with me forever and makes me seethe with jealousy and fear and love for my wife, who may never be that again.

There is nothing for it but to wait. Never have I felt so powerless. Never so despairing. I fear that she is in danger, yet she has resisted my every attempt to help her. If there is right in this world, she will return to me. That is my only hope.

Ch. 37

Dear Jane,

I know you think me vain and heartless and I will confess to you that you are half right. Heartless I am not. It is just that my heart belongs, or should I say belonged, to Colonel Millar. All that I was belonged to him. Until now. I hope you are seated safely in a sturdy chair, for in this letter I will relate to you the manner in which my world came to an end.

After Mr. Bennet's departure from Bath, I was of course distraught and could not keep from sobbing so loudly and so long that several of the servants hastened to my room to enquire if they could be of help. I shook my head and recommenced my wailing, for what, dear Jane, had I done but turn away my own husband! Such overwhelming guilt was new to me, though I am sure you would opine that by this time guilt surely must be a constant companion. Much of my lament, however, centered on my colonel, for what could I hope from him now, after Mr. Bennet had accosted him in so ungentlemanly a fashion, reminding him that I was a married woman? Most likely he would choose never again to seek my company, a thought that returned me once more to undiminished weeping.

I turned to Mrs. Littleworth for comfort and advice. She was ever so understanding; indeed, she was like a mother to me just then. "Leave everything to me," she said. "All is not lost." And away she went to a destination unnamed.

Soon enough she returned and said, "Colonel Millar will be at the New Assembly Rooms tomorrow at five o'clock in the afternoon. He has secured a private corner for tea in the octagon room. He begs you to meet him there, where, he asserts, your conversation will be undisturbed."

Saved! All was not lost! Undeserving as I was, I was to be given another chance for a new life.

"Now, dry your tears. Much will have to be done to repair the damage your weeping has done to your face. Thank heaven for colour; we shall have to apply considerably more if you are to be an object of desire."

I wrapped my arms around her ample self and wept anew, this time from happiness, from gratitude for being given a second chance—or was it a third? I had decided long ago not to keep count. Fortunately I was brought suddenly to my senses by a concern of the utmost importance: what should I wear?

That night I could barely sleep for imagining myself in which one, of all the fine gowns Mrs. Littleworth had so thoughtfully and generously provided, I would be most alluring. And then it came to me. Ah yes! I would appear as much as possible like the girl from Meryton, the innocent young thing he found so irresistible. Surely then he would recall our first meeting, and the stage would be set for revealing the identity of his child, my little Jane. I would arrange myself to look demure yet delightful, untouched but touchable.

I chose a simple white chemise, thin and flowing, gathered with a narrow blue ribbon beneath my breasts. I would carry a cashmere shawl to protect my shoulders from the cool air of evening or to give myself a hint of mystery should I decide to wear it over my curls. I would wear my hair down with only a thin blue ribbon as ornament. Mrs. Littleworth urged me to be generous with colour for my lips and cheeks, but I demurred, dashing only a bit onto my cheeks and biting my lips to bring forth the natural colour that was mine. I was a breath of springtime in the autumn of the year. Who could resist me?

I can hear now, dear sister, your sharp intake of breath, can feel your wanting to have me before you so that you can scold me for my prideful foolishness. Fret no more, my comeuppance is nigh.

The colonel and I dined discreetly in a lovely alcove just off the octagon room, which offered the privacy rarely available in the gathering places of Bath. No Grand Concourse for us, not as we planned our escape from humdrum convention and tiresome society. We sipped Champagne—it had become my favourite French *eau*—and his eyes met mine. "Soon we will be together," he said. He reached for my hand.

Jane, I am approaching that part of the evening which is most upsetting to me. You will find much of this letter blotted with tears, but I must go on. I have heard it said that confession is good for the soul but I beg to disagree. Confession is the shredding of the soul accompanied by pain indescribable by my poor pen. Bear with me, I beg of you, please know that I am suffering.

"We are together now," I teased my captain. "What can you mean?" I pulled my hand away.

"I mean that I shall hold you close, that you will be mine." He moved nearer to me and took my hand once again. I could feel his breath on my neck. I shivered as a most sudden and now familiar feeling surged deep within me. I felt my face flush; my breath came quickly.

"Forever," I breathed.

"Forever."

I felt his warm lips on my neck just below my ear. They glided gently down and fell into the hollow of my shoulder. I feared I was about to swoon. "Oh please," I begged. "Allow me to catch my breath. I am feeling faint."

He released me but still held me close. He handed me my little blue hair ribbon, which had slipped to my shoulders as he wooed me, and I felt at that moment that he would look after me forever. I knew that my refusal to return to home and family was the right thing to do. I knew that this man cared for me in a way that my husband never could. I knew that my marriage and my life at Longbourn were wrong. I knew that the colonel and I were meant to be together and marriage be damned. Was ever a girl so misguided!

Our room had emptied itself of other visitors. Teatime had come and gone. The tables were bare except for the china cups holding the dregs of some exotic tea and a few plates sullied with bits of cucumber and watercress. Evening was becoming night.

"Please," I begged. "May we not walk a bit? It is so very warm in here." Indeed, my cheeks felt afire.

"Of course, my love. Let us repair to the out-of-doors. The cover of night will provide us with all the privacy we need." He rose from the table and led me out to the deserted gardens nearby. "You are so lovely, my dearest one. Your flush becomes you. It makes you so very alive, my darling."

None of this was cooling. I leaned against him and begged, "Please, find a bench where we might sit for a moment until I regain my composure." And the strength of my lower limbs, I could have added, for they had turned to warm milk and I feared I might fall.

"Come, my darling," he said. "I have rooms not far from here. Are you agreeable to accompanying me there?"

"Yes."

Thus began the night I had longed for, the night that would change my life forever.

I cannot tell you what his rooms were like nor even where they were located. I remember only standing stock-still while he kissed me on my mouth and my eyes and at the same time began to unfasten my dress, which quite naturally fell from my shoulders. But impediments showed themselves: never before had I hated my underthings, but now, what with the loosening and untying and struggling with twisted ribbons and laces, even so patient a lover as my colonel began to mutter his frustration, and for a brief moment I considered taking myself into my own hands, when at last he succeeded in unfastening my corset and then my chemise, thus rendering me naked to my waist. I stood like a statue, feeling his hot breath upon my neck and then my shoulders and upon my breasts as all the while he held me around the waist so that I would not faint dead away. He kissed me where no one had gone before. "You are so lovely," he murmured and took my nipple into his mouth. At this I felt myself melting; I could barely breathe and feared that I would crumple to the ground. He laid me carefully upon the velvet covering of his couch, which, in retrospect, had surely felt the weight of many a woman, but which at the time felt designed just for me. And then, with his mouth upon my breasts and then my belly, somewhat flattened, thank goodness, by my horizontal position, and then so close to the mound of my womanhood, he said, "At last, I have you. Remove your shoes." As my shoes were all that were left of my original habiliments I kicked them to the floor, where they joined the rest of my clothing there in a heap, and I did so without the slightest protest and with all the speed that I could muster. "You are so lovely," he murmured. The oceans swelled within me and I welcomed him in. Glorious surrender.

I can write no more just now.

M.

But I must.

Afterward, we lay quietly together, each of us lost in our own thoughts, each of us feeling the quietude that surely must come after so passionate an interlude. I thought to ease us into a bit of conversation, and so I said, "May I enquire into a matter of some import to me?"

"Anything, my adored one."

"Please do not think me forward, but I cannot call you Colonel, not after we have been so intimate. What is your given name, dearest?" He was silent. To encourage him, I asked, "What, for instance, does your sister call you?"

"What my sister calls me is of no matter here," he said abruptly and rose from the couch.

"Oh please, I did not mean to offend, but if we are to—"

"Yes, yes, of course." He paced back and forth for a

moment and then said, "You can call me Charles, my darling. Indeed, I would like to hear you say my name."

"Charles," I murmured. In my mind's eye I saw my future calling cards: "Mrs. Charles Millar." I heard our names announced at banquets and balls: "Colonel and Mrs. Millar." So much more dignified than "Mr. and Mrs. Bennet." Oh, what a nuisance, my husband. But not such an obstacle as one might suppose, for I have heard tell of persons who journeyed to America to begin a new life. My colonel and I could do the same. We could start afresh with none of the archaic conventions that hinder the blossoming of our life together in this country. The world is so full of a wonder of things; why should we not avail ourselves of them? I can think of no good reason.

Charles sat himself upon the couch once more. I felt the heat rise in me again. "And Charles, my dearest, what shall you call me? You know, endearments alone may not prove sufficient in all instances of our life together. Our long life together," I added.

Again he rose but now I felt a coolness. He paced and I grew cold. "My darling," he said, "my endearments will never grow stale, nor will they ever be diluted of their passion. Passion for you, my darling."

"Oh, Charles, you are so wonderful. Still"—and here I knew I was taking my life into my hands—"I remain curious. What, should the necessity arise, will you call me? What is my name, dear heart?"

His face paled, though handsomely, and he took up his pacing once more. I began to fear I had been too bold; perhaps I should have waited until we were Colonel and Mrs. Millar before broaching so private a conversation. Suddenly he stopped his pacing and turned to face me, his colour fully restored, and said in the most *charmant* manner, "Lydia. I shall call you Lydia." Lydia? My face must have fallen for he rushed to add, "No matter what your name really is you will be Lydia to me and only to me. It is our little secret. No one else but the two of us shall know. My darling."

The two of us. My heart was full to bursting. *Our little secret.* I sat up from the couch and threw my arms around his neck. "Oh, Charles."

"Now, now, my dear," he said, unwinding me from himself. "We must be cautious until such time—"

"Until such time as . . . ?" I could not wait for his answer and so I said, "Until such time as we are man and wife."

He stiffened then and said somewhat condescendingly, "Do you not remember that you are already married? Do you not recall that unpleasant little man who so rudely interrupted our tête-à-tête—"

"Tetatet, what is that?"

Impatiently, he answered, "It's French, but never mind."

"But I do mind. What does it mean?"

"I fail to understand how you can be so scattered in your conversation. Furthermore, I hate being interrupted. I find it quite disconcerting. However, since you insist, it's French for 'face-to-face.' Lydia," he added.

Lydia. What a lovely sound, what a lovely name. I would endeavour to do better. "I will endeavour to do better," I said. "And yes, I do recall Mr. Bennet's appearance and behaviour and my chagrin over both. He had no right, no right at all."

Charles looked puzzled. "But, my darling, he is your lawful husband."

"Lawful, that is all. And none of that matters. You will be my true husband."

"Of course, but we need not concern ourselves with that now."

Something in me compelled me to the notion, however dangerous, that now was the time to plan for the future. "Where will we live, my dearest?" I asked in my most timid fashion.

"Never fear. Perhaps somewhere near the sea, perhaps upon a hillock in a dale, perhaps in a teeming city, perhaps simply beneath the open skies. What need have we of shelter? We have our love."

With that, he drew me to him, placed his finger beneath my chin, and raised my face to his for a solemn kiss, his solemn promise that we two would be joined forever.

"But"—he wagged his finger at me—"wherever we

live it will not be here. So we must make plans to leave Bath. Soon is not soon enough for me, for I must have more of you."

Now I decided was the perfect time to introduce his little daughter to him. I would need to use the utmost caution; after all, little Jane would be a great shock to even so worldly a man as my colonel. Once he became accustomed to his newly discovered fatherhood, we would be We Three and my dream would come true.

Charles by now had dressed himself and I followed suit. I did not want to leave these rooms, not ever, but sensing some impatience in him, I said, "Shall we walk a bit?"

Night was giving way to day. We strolled along the river, which by now barely mirrored the moon. I held Charles's arm; he covered my hand with his. I granted him yet another kiss and then begged to be seated. Charles found the perfect bench. Behind us the leaves of the trees rustled, then fell to the ground, creating a canopy of reds and golds and yellows. The time was right. Loosing myself from his affectionate grasp, I said, "Charles, my darling, what thoughts have you about children?"

"They are fine, just so long as they keep their distance. Why do you ask?"

This was not a propitious beginning. "Oh, no reason," I said as airily as I could. "Can you imagine our creating a family"—here I stuttered—"a child or perhaps two who would carry on your name?" He stiffened. "And care for Northfield in your dotage?"

"I do not intend to suffer a dotage. I shall most likely fall in battle before that."

I uttered a little shriek. "Dear heart! Say not so!"

"What is all this, then, about children? My duties as a military man preclude children. Furthermore, as you have been quick to celebrate, We Two will do just fine. Something awkward about We Three or, God help us, We Four. Let us continue our stroll."

"No, no, dear, just a moment longer." I swear, sister, the wind grew stronger and colder. The river had turned from black to silver. Day was upon us. "Charles," I said, "please hear me out."

"What is it?" His impatience was showing.

"We are already We Three."

"Silly goose, come now; let us find a warmer spot. Better yet, let us head for my carriage. It is past your bedtime, my darling. Besides, I have made my feelings clear: I have never cared much for children. To be blunt, I do not care one whit for them. Now, shall we go?"

This was it, all or nothing: "My dear, you would care for one such child, if you knew her."

"Surely we could find some sort of conversation pleasing to us both. This one is boring me to distraction."

Nothing, not even his boredom, could stop me now. "Do you recall the child you thought so adorable at the village fair? The child you called lovely? Her name is Jane. She is two years old. She was born nine months after you and I met. She is your daughter, yours and mine."

"Silence!" he ordered. "It is not fitting for a married woman to have so intimate an exchange with a man not her husband."

"She is your child, my beloved. Jane belongs to you."

"Nonsense! This cannot be." He rose as if to leave.

I rushed on. "We could easily pass by Longbourn and collect her. She is our child. She is our life together."

His response was instantaneous and as I look back, probably not the first time he had uttered it: "And how could I be certain of that? Given the wanton behaviour you have apprised me of, your child's father could be any one of a number of men, men whom you have deceived just as you have deceived me, as you have deceived your husband. I cannot abide deceit. You have besmirched my honour."

"I? I have besmirched your honour? What about mine?"

"You have no honour, madam, not now, not ever."

"None now that you revile me." I fell on my knees and beseeched him, "Have pity, my love."

"Get up, you fool," he ordered. "Someone may see us." And with that he jerked me upright. "You have misled me. Damn you."

I stared into the darkness at his retreating back and thought of how I might shoot it. From this distance my beloved looked more like a rabbit caught in a hunter's sights than a man. Yet he need not have feared me. Had I had a firearm I would not have had the strength to raise it, let alone to fire it. I stared into the empty darkness until the chill of the early morning, so cold as to deny the sun forever, forced me to rise from the odious bench, and somehow I managed to stumble back to Mrs. Littleworth's rooms.

Fortunately, my friend and protector was engaged at the gaming tables and I was free to weep as loudly as ever I have or wish to again. My fury was not just at the colonel. My anger was at myself. How could I have been so foolish? How could I have let that man take such liberties? Where was I to go now? What life was left to me? I was and am deeply ashamed and I shall remain so all the rest of my life.

Upon Mrs. Littleworth's return, I threw myself upon her and sobbed anew. "What is it, child?" she asked. "Here, here, dry your eyes. Tell your mum everything."

So I did. "And he deserted me. He walked away and left me alone there in the darkness, all alone without protection or friendship or anything at all except his never-ending loathing of me, his own dear one, his own Lydia!"

"Good God, I am ruined!" said Mrs. Littleworth. "Did he say where he was going?"

"He said nothing. But why, pray tell, are you ruined? It is I who am ruined!"

Mrs. Littleworth's face contorted itself in a way I had never seen. "Where do you think the money came from, for your wardrobe, your coiffeur, your face, your complete transformation into a lady of Society? Your dancing master, your French tutor—expenses I incurred gladly and for your benefit. And now what have you done? All my hard work arranging for meetings, reserving rooms, encouraging walks and talks, all for nothing. I will be cast out in the morning if not before." She turned her back on me and sailed toward the door. "One last piece of advice," she said. "You had best be gone within the day. You have failed me, you little fool."

Another shock, dear Jane, as if I were being lashed anew. My friend and confidante had turned against me. I was indeed alone as I had never before been. Perhaps this most recent shock dried my tears, but dried they were and I sat there wondering how the tragedy of my life concerned Mrs. Littleworth.

I brushed past Mrs. Littleworth's maid and burst into her boudoir. "I demand to know," I said. "What do you mean by 'cast out'? What has that to do with our friendship, your kindness, your generosity to me?"

"Just who do you think your benefactor was? Mr. Littleworth? Hah! My husband cut off my funds weeks ago, shortly after we arrived."

So Mr. Bennet was right; Mr. Littleworth had rendered her penniless. "And so you are without funds?"

"It pleases Mr. Littleworth to think me so. But I am not without funds. I have not been without funds for quite some time. Mr. Littleworth's money was but a drop in the pond required to make you socially acceptable."

"Then who? The colonel?"

"Colonel Millar's attentions to you were my doing. I

arranged not only for meetings and for your walks about this town and for the balls in the evening and for—"

"But my gowns! My shoes! My lessons! Where did that money come from if not from the colonel?" As much as I hated to admit it, he seemed the most likely source.

Mrs. Littleworth rose from her settee and puffed herself up to a great expanse. "The money came from me. All of it, every pound, every shilling, came from me."

"From you? You have been so very kind to me, but I cannot think that your affection for me would cost you so dearly." The light was dawning. "In return for?"

"In return for you. You, my dear, provided the protection I needed."

I was becoming even more confused. "Protection from what?"

"I was to deliver you to him dressed like a lady with the manners of a lady but with the yearning of a woman. And, now that we are about it, why do you think I dressed you in so unusual a fashion, a veritable curtain overflowing your ever-burgeoning belly? I could not chance that he would reject you should he discover your swelling, you his virginal country girl. Because, you silly goose, do not suppose that you are his only one. He fills his time with all sorts of women, you offering the greatest challenge given that you are married. Perhaps it is your stupidity as well that attracts him. Perhaps he hoped that your motherhood would make you even more of a challenge, that's all. But of course you with your simpering ways turned out to be no challenge whatsoever; no wonder he fled. With very little cause, he could have deserted us both long ago had I not been so vigilant and industrious on your behalf. And now he has! Thanks to you!"

I gasped; every word she uttered took the breath from me. "And you!" I sputtered. "You carried out your part of the bargain. How can you then be ruined? Surely you are owed! By him!"

"We will never see him again. Oh yes, he would have snatched you away to some destination known only to him, and I suspect he would have tossed you out once he'd had his fill of you. But by then I would have departed the scene with savings enough to assure my return to the tables wherever and whenever I wished. But not now, you strumpet! Do you not know, you idiot child, that you provide a cover for me?"

I stared at her, dumbstruck. What can she mean, a cover? I did feel, at that moment, like an idiot child, so like an idiot child I began to weep.

"Stop your bloody crying," Mrs. Littleworth ordered. "You are no good to me now. To think of the money I spent on you just so that I would have good reason to appear in Bath sans husband and in the gaming rooms, my true destination. As long as you were visible, I could appear the chaperone, the friend, the protector you thought I was and be received in the most respectable homes during visiting hours. At night you would be holding hands with the colonel, thus freeing me to apply my talents elsewhere in a place where no one, not even the cleverest card-player, would think to question my estimable presence at the tables."

Here she must have called up a pleasing reminiscence, as a smile appeared on her face. I took heart. "You used me," I said. "You betrayed me."

"Of course I did, and I would have continued to do so had you not pushed yourself forward like the peasant you are. You are not the first innocent I have shepherded into Society, though you will likely be my last. You with your nattering on about children. Why couldn't you have slowed things? Good heavens, one kiss and you are ready to throw your entire life into the gutter—and mine—for a few hours of what you call love. How could you have been so stupid?"

She moved toward me as if to strike me. I covered my head with my hands and said, as if to assure her that I had learned her lesson, "I am stupid no longer."

"Only a few more nights and I would have made off with a fortune," she said, "and with it, I would have gained entry into the grandest houses in England. Such a future I envisioned! Fleecing the highest, the most noble, the richest denizens in the land! My dream would have come true. And now? Now word of this will get out and I will be persona non grata at every table in the country. Drat! And with the London season just beginning. Thanks to you, I am left with no season at all!"

By now she stood towering over me and once more I begged. "O Mrs. Littleworth, take pity on me," I said. "I, too, am left with nothing."

What an ugly laugh! I glanced up to see her wide-open mouth. How could I have failed to notice the absence of all those teeth before now? She leaned down to me, her bosom heaving this way and that, and bellowed, "You deserve every bit of suffering that has come to you, you useless piece of baggage. You brought about your own downfall—and mine. And now? I am left with demands from every tradesman, every dressmaker, every ribboner in town. I will be penniless before dawn. And all because of you, a stupid little tramp."

"I am stupid no longer." It was all I could think of to say, and so I said it over and over until finally she swept from the room.

Dear Jane, if there is anything to be gained from this terrible time, perhaps it is that though I would gladly have done without it, the shock forced me to see my world as it is: my love a prowler upon the innocent, a black-hearted reprobate, a wicked man; my friend, my confidante a liar, a panderer, a pimp, a procurer of flesh, just as if I were a scarlet woman in some bordello. I count myself fortunate to have been cast from such a society. Why, then, am I so miserable?

And I am with child. No, not the colonel's, thank heaven. I am carrying little Edward's twin. I had thought that the cessation of my flow was caused by the miscarriage or by the grief thereafter. I had thought that my burgeoning belly was the result of my childish desires for sweets and butters. I had, if I am to tell the truth, not thought at all, perhaps not for most of my life. But I must begin now. I will write Mr. Bennet. I will go home where I belong. I will beg him to forgive my foolish wandering with that blackguard, though of course I will not apprise him of the extent of the liberties I allowed the cad to take. I beg you to keep my secrets, in particular that of little Jane's paternity. In return, I promise to become a faithful wife and a peerless mother. You will be proud of me. And perhaps I will, too.

Ch. 38

October of '87

Dear Husband,

I shall return to you within the week. It seems that you were correct: Mrs. Littleworth has mounted such losses at the gaming tables that Mr. Littleworth stopped her credit. She is furious with him but not as furious as I suspect he is with her. Penury is not in her nature so she is closing up the house and returning, so I assume, to her husband. And I will take my proper place next to you and my children.

I look forward to my homecoming. My girls must be ever so grown and I am determined to be the mother they deserve and hope for. With that in mind, I shall make extra efforts on behalf of Elizabeth, who, as you know, has not been much in my favour. I shall change all that.

Now I hope you are sitting down, for what I am about to tell you will come as a shock, a pleasant one, I hope. I am bringing you an unexpected gift. I am carrying your child, our little Edward's twin. I had not known until a few days ago but find myself quite happy that little Edward will be with us by way of his sister or brother. I do hope it is a boy. You would be so pleased, I know. I am most desperate to keep this baby safe within. I cannot lose this child, nor any child. I pray each night that I may keep him safe. I love this child already and cannot wait for his arrival—or hers—in December.

I long to take my rightful place as

Your Wife,
Marianne.

Ch. 39

A man may shoot the man who invades his character,
as he may shoot him who attempts to break into his house.

—SAMUEL JOHNSON

My wife thinks that with her sweet note all will be forgiven and we will resume life as a married couple. She thinks that to present me with her unborn child will make amends for her behaviour. She thinks to pass off this latest child as mine. She is wrong on all counts. I have not forgiven her. Nor will I ever forget the humiliation heaped upon me when, in Bath, she tore herself from my grasp and raced after that bounder, leaving me to stand in the middle of the path, a figure of scorn should anyone venture past, a husband abandoned in a public place by a wife whose contumely knew no bounds. Unsuccessful in her attempt to throw herself into the arms of her lover, did she then return with me to Mrs. Littleworth's of her own free will? No. Was she successful in her attempt to seduce me into allowing her to stay in Bath? No. Did she return with me at that moment to her rightful home? No. And so, at the end of my encounter during which I attempted to show her the folly of her ways, I had no recourse but to leave the premises and make the sad and dreary journey back to Longbourn.

I had been shown to be a man without honour, a cuckold, a worthless appendage to a woman who had abandoned her husband and her children and her place as a respectable woman in society. What could I possibly do to repair such damage?

I had not held a firearm since my youth. My father, thinking to teach me manly habits, took me often into the woods where we sought to flush out a few grouse. He showed me his gun, how to load it, and where to fire it. I did so, though without much enthusiasm, for I had no quarrel with birds and small animals, and grouse was not much good for eating anyway. So I paid as little attention to the workings of firearms as I could get away with, reminding myself to call out "Good shot!" every time I heard the crack of my father's gun.

As for pistols—those instruments integral to dueling now that swords, thanks to the vagary of fashion, had fallen from favour—I was quite unacquainted with them save to look at them in Father's study where they lay side by side upon a bed of velvet within an oaken case. Fortunately, or so it would seem now, Tom, when only a boy like me, took it upon himself to show me the rudiments of pistol shooting, and together we would borrow the pistols, unloaded, of course, and play at being highwaymen. Great fun as I recall.

The venture I was about to undertake would be not at all amusing nor would it be for sport. I could be killed. I could kill another. What price honour?

And so the duel. If I could not restore Marianne's reputation, I could, with luck, restore mine.

Tom was not at all enthusiastic about being my second. "Surely, sir, there is a less dangerous way to settle a dispute." I would have none of it, yet he continued his argument. "But, sir, I know nothing about dueling." I answered that he knew enough about pistols to give me some reassurance that I would not make a fool out of myself. To that, he agreed. I made my way to Northfield, where, only a few days before, the colonel had made his return. Heedless of his servant's "I will see if the master is at home," I brushed him aside and stomped into the sitting room. "Millar! Edward Bennet here. I come to call you out!"

Millar drew himself up from the chair he had been sitting in. "Surely you jest," he said.

I threw my glove on the floor. "There," I said, "the die is cast. Choose your weapons."

I had never before seen such insolence as in the way he stood, in the way he looked at me—a veritable curl in his lip—and in the languid way he picked up the glove. "You cannot be serious," he said. "I am after all a military man and am accomplished in the way of weapons and, if the truth be known, dueling."

"I am well aware of your history, all of it," I said. "Choose your weapons. Our seconds will agree on a time and place."

"Now, hold on, my man. If you are set upon shooting someone, you might turn your attention to that idiot woman who is your wife. She is a silly creature, a mere trifle, surely not so worthy as to warrant our discommoding ourselves in so dramatic a fashion." He bowed slightly. "Be assured that I return her to you with the same alacrity with which she left you. You have my sympathy."

I repeated, "Choose your weapons."

He smiled, again the curled lip. "As you wish. Pistols."

"Pistols it shall be. Good morning to you."

And thus it was that on an overcast morning, the light of day just beginning to show through the forest, we two found ourselves selecting pistols, readying ourselves for what could be the last hour of our lives. Our seconds stood nearby. Tom looked wary. The colonel's second, a lowly private—could he find no one of his class friendly to his cause?—looked terrified.

As for the colonel, he had dressed himself in full military regalia no doubt to intimidate me into withdrawing from an exercise that he considered beneath him. "'Tis not too late, Bennet, to save ourselves this trouble and return to our warm beds."

"It is too late. You have impugned my honour and sullied the reputation of my wife."

"I know nothing of your honour, but the reputation of your wife, such as you put it, is her own doing. And yours, if I may be so bold. A husband who cannot control his wife has only himself to blame for her excursions into questionable territory. I have nothing to do with any of this foolishness."

"You are a coward, Millar. All your talk is nothing but an attempt to save your own hide, but this time your slick tongue will not protect you. I will have my satisfaction. Proceed, Tom."

Tom read out the rules from the pamphlet I had secured from my library, placed there long ago I expect by my father. "You will, after choosing your pistol, walk thirty paces in the direction opposite to the other. You will turn, then, and on my signal, you will fire. Once. Is that agreed?"

We nodded, each took up one of the pistols, and glanced briefly at one another. It gave me great pleasure to see that Colonel Millar was not quite so haughty now; after all, he could not know for certain my level of expertise with firearms, but he could be certain of my seriousness. This, he knew finally, was not a joke.

I turned my back, he turned his, and I walked thirty paces toward the dawn. We turned. Tom tossed his neckerchief onto the ground, our signal to fire. We faced each other and aimed. I felt the shot sting my breast. I fell, certain that this breath would be my last. As I lay there on the cold grey ground where sunlight would never again show itself, a truth, as if it were a bullet itself, struck me: that honour is a poxy whore, my wife is wicked, the world is wicked, and I am wicked. I took my hand from my chest expecting blood to gush forth and not caring that it would. My life—not an especially distinguished one—was quite over. It was of little matter that my existence ended in such a ridiculous way, a bullet bleeding the life out of me. I readied myself to sigh a final good-bye when just at that moment, Tom reached beneath my torn shirt to ascertain the extent and the site of the wound, and to his amazement and mine, he pulled forth my pocket edition of Montaigne, its cover shot through. "You are saved, sir," said Tom. "A miracle."

To the astonishment of my opponent and of the hapless private, I rose unsteadily to my feet and said with all the force of one so nearly dead, "Stand, sir, and be fired upon." Colonel Millar did as I demanded and in his eyes I read more fear than contempt. He all but turned away entirely, perhaps intending even to run. What a waste of a man, I thought. He is not worth the powder. Nor is she. I have risked my life for a woman who can never love me, nor I her, but to whom I am forever bound. I am about to shoot a man who is of no import to me, who is incidental to the downward spiral of my life, no matter that I stand here unharmed. And with that and out of pure disgust I raised my pistol and fired into the air. What little satisfaction was to be gained from this ridiculous situation was now mine. Quite amazing how little it mattered. Then, like the wounded man I was expected to be, I fell once more to the ground.

When the smoke cleared, the colonel exclaimed, "My God! What can have happened? I did not mean to wound you." He stood transfixed, holding the revolver, while the private, now as pale as his commanding officer, raced to aid Tom, who by this time had wrapped his neckerchief about my breast. "The pistol, something must have gone awry with the weapon. It aimed where I would not have it. It is not my fault! I will not have it so!"

"He thinks you are wounded, sir," Tom whispered. Millar continued from his position sixty paces away: "Please forgive the poor aim," he shouted. "I never meant to hit you; I meant only to frighten you." I groaned loudly. Millar babbled on: "We must keep all this a secret; no one must know." Tom shot him a look far more dangerous than any bullet. "Afraid we can't do that, sir. This man needs medical attention."

Millar covered his face and his voice shook: "And now my reputation as an officer and a gentleman—and yes, as an excellent shot—is ruined." I pretended to struggle to stand, then to lose my balance, steadied by Tom and the private. "Good going, sir," said Tom. "We're with ye," said the private.

"Private! Stand here with me!" the colonel ordered. The private did not move. "Oh, God," Millar moaned.

"Good grief, now I am deserted, and soon everyone will know that only I fired at my opponent and that you, you damned commoner, shot into the air. Everyone will believe that you are the gentleman and I the cad." With that he fell to his knees and, in the presence of his inferiors, began to weep.

Glorious surrender. Satisfaction is mine. My honour is restored. I care not a jot.

Ah yes, of course, at home and with my dutiful wife, another scene: "What has happened?" she shrieked. "You are filthy, your boots muddy to the knee! Oh, what is that hole in your jacket? Why is such a hole . . ." Apparently she realized that a gunshot might do that sort of damage because she began to tear at my coat. "Take it off! Get it away from here! What has happened? No, do not tell me! Who is dead? Do not tell me! Are you hurt?" And on and on. She whirled about the room, shrieking for the servants, plucking first at myself and then at the draperies and the lace coverings on the chairs, all the while dancing further and further away from my disordered appearance. Ah yes, my wife has returned. And as expected, she is of little use. I shrugged off my jacket and proceeded into my library from where I write this entry.

She adds to my household another child, a boy, I hope, but if not, a girl will do. The parentage of such a child will always remain a mystery, at least to me, but she or I hope he will be welcome in my house nonetheless. Whichever its sex, it will always remain a stranger to me; indifference is preferable to cruelty, and I have no need of the latter. Although still babies, Jane and Elizabeth have become company quite delightful enough, I suppose, in their own though different ways. They scoot about the house, Elizabeth crawling behind Jane as together they sing songs taught them by Mathilda, she who is now mercifully absent.

My intention is to ignore my wife's dalliance. In that, I am certain to be successful, for I no longer care that she may have gone even so far as to give herself to another. She will not have the satisfaction of knowing of the duel; she would of course make herself the heroine of whatever transpired. She may hear of it from others, but as for me, I have lost interest in her, in most everything. As for myself, I have no plans to confess my sins to Mrs. Bennet. After all, I owe her less than what I have already given her. Mrs. Rummidge has no reason to suspect that my behaviour with the serving wench went beyond mere talk, and of course my little girls have quite forgot what they never quite knew. I am safe. It is good to be safe; I shall not risk losing myself again.

I have decided on names for this child. If it is a boy, he shall be called Thomas after my friend, who will be pleased by such an honour. If it is a girl, she shall be called Mary after my wife, by whom I intend to be well pleased, exactly as a husband deserves and whenever he desires. I have discussed these names with Mrs. Rummidge and she has given her blessing. It is time that my household experience a peacefulness unknown in recent years. It is time that everyone calms down and tends to the duties at hand. I will see to it, mark my words.

And so I set this journal aside, perhaps forever. The need for confession seems to have passed and in its place comes the sort of contentment I have not experienced in these many months. It may be that in the future, should circumstances dictate, I will take up this pen once more. For now, though, my tale is ended. I shall withdraw into the saving graces of my books.

Ch. 40

Dear Jane,

I had not been home for even a fortnight when on an early morning my husband burst through the front door looking for all the world as if he had been in a battle! His coat was torn, he wore some sort of bandage around his chest, his trousers and boots were covered with mud; and what is worse, he would not tell me what occurred that would leave him in such disrepair! I did what I could, trying to snatch the doilies from the chairs to clean him as best I could, but he seemed not at all interested in his own well-being or in my concern. He simply walked past me and into his library, where, I am duty-bound to admit, he spends more and more of his time. Thus, I have had to set my curiosity aside, for I know that he will never confide in me. A most private man, my husband.

No matter all that, I am here at Longbourn now a

month and ready to endure—this time without protest—another birth of the child I pray is a boy, my lost Edward's brother. It shall be soon.

Mr. Bennet received me politely despite my long absence and my wrongdoings, such as he understands them. His attentions to me have been cordial, though not as warm as I would wish. In return, I have exerted myself to become the sort of wife who deserves his respect. To wit, I rise with the sun each day, dress without the assistance of a maid, and see to my children even before their nurse is awake. Oh, Jane, they are wonderful, my girls. Elizabeth, about whom you have heard so much, most of it off-putting, has come round and holds out her little hands and says "Mama" so beautifully and then smiles and toddles to me and I lift her into my arms and hold her close. Little Jane comes stumbling after and soon we are entwined, the three of us. Not all the perfume from Arabia could smell as sweet as my children.

For a brief time we play their favourite game, One-Two, Buckle My Shoe, which you surely remember from our own childhood. My babies will learn numbers and counting from me just as they are learning words from all those around them. I do believe that girls need to acquire skills of management, in addition to the sewing and preserving of fruits, which, while taught us by our mother, were neglected while I was away. I find it painful to write the word Bath, for it summons memories I would prefer to forget just as I am trying to forget the girl I pretended to be during those weeks, my mortification so near at hand that I could not see it. Thus, I think of that time as "when I was away."

I have given up French. In the early days of my return, Mr. Bennet thought to please me with the little French he knew, although his tone was not at all cheery, more sarcastic, more like what I sometimes heard from the wags in Bath. I have asked him to leave off "ma cherie" and stick to "Mrs. Bennet" and, if he so chooses, "my dear." Recently he has so chosen. Why anyone would prefer French to English is beyond me, given that the country—France, that is—is in such constant turmoil. They cannot keep a king or even a queen, it seems, and talk is everywhere about some horrific tool of execution the French invented, *la guillotine*. Fortunately, I have forsworn the language so am not bothered to discover just what it is. I note only that it is female; only the French would be so bold, although surely they would not be so bold as to make use of it.

I have taken over the Family Accounts, you will be pleased to know. Mr. Bennet was at first unsure about my becoming Treasurer but I convinced him that his leisure time would only increase and so he acceded to my pleas, though only for what he calls a trial period. So far I have done a fine job. Even Mr. Bennet agrees, though somewhat distantly. I continue to assist the housekeeper in the making of jellies, comfits, sweetmeats, and cordials and will continue to do so until the child within demands that I give all my attention to him. I have begun to look about me, at the village and persons there less fortunate than I, and I find that my visits to the sick and the poor are welcome. I shall continue my efforts on their behalf once my lying-in period is behind me.

As if to acknowledge the improvements I have made in myself, Mr. Bennet, during a moment of unexpected intimacy, when it appeared that my about-to-be-born would indeed become born, uttered a somewhat odd promise: that he would accept the child as his be it a girl or a boy. If it is a boy, he wishes to name him Tom. If it is a girl, he wishes to name her Mary, after yours truly. I am quite overcome, though I remain a bit puzzled.

Nonetheless, dear sister, I am making an effort to do my duty. I accept that at eighteen I am a woman, a girl no longer. I acknowledge that I am the mother of two and soon of three. Happily, I am the wife of a virtuous man. I have put my girlish past behind me and find that I do not miss it. But oh, Jane, all this is easier to write than to live. There are moments when a thrill passes through me, when I recall the touch of his hand, of his lips on mine, of the passion that surged from deep within my very being. I have found in myself that which heretofore I believed to simmer only in men and which I know must be stilled. To that end, I have taken to placing a pebble in my shoe. As I walk, it rubs uncomfortably against the heel and serves to remind me of my fall—or should I say falls—from grace. It is a daily, albeit minimal, punishment. However, I shall keep all that to myself as I see no reason to share with Mr. Bennet the secrets that I must carry to my grave. Little Jane will belong to him always, as will I. 'Tis enough. 'Twill do.

Your devoted sister,
Mrs. Edward Bennet

Ch. 41

Summum nec metuas diem, nec optes.

"Neither to wish, nor fear, to die."

—MARTIAL

I had thought to be finished with Montaigne, but such changes, sudden and unpredictable, have driven me to seek understanding and comfort in one wiser than I.

In the beginning, once Mrs. Bennet had healed from her delivery of little Mary, I had thought to take my pleasure in my wife's bedchamber. At first this was so, and she behaved much as her letter to me had promised. She was a doting mother to all three of our children. She took on the management of the household and even some of the duties. I could hear her humming in the kitchen as she went about preserving fruits and vegetables. I could hear Cook humming with her. She took over the accounts and did so beautifully; I of course checked her calculations and records, all done in her beautiful hand, and found no fault, no errors. But with the coming of spring she changed. She withdrew from the kitchen. She insisted I hire a wet nurse for Mary and Elizabeth and a governess for Jane, who to my mind is not ready for any such person. And she returned the accounts books to me.

Oh yes, she smiled agreeably enough. She never turned me out of her bedroom. She acquiesced to my husbandly demands, and here, too, I must record a change: heretofore, especially in the early days of our marriage, Mrs. Bennet as good as pushed me from her bed postcoitus; she could not wait for me to depart her room. More recently, my experience has been markedly different: she has insisted that I am to remain aware of the presence of both persons during the time of conjugation; to that end and to prevent an uproar, I am diligent in my attempts to murmur sweet nothings, to be gentle at the time of entrance, and, afterward, to remain abed, to speak affectionately to her—"You are lovely," she has ordered me to say—and above all, to stay awake; about the latter, she is adamant. Much as it seems that falling asleep is the perfectly natural thing to do after exertion of such magnitude, I have learned that doing so arouses the ire of my wife, that one is obliged to have a bit of a chat; and so I strain to stay awake and chatting until such time as I am excused. I must say, it is difficult to fashion a chat with only one person, in this case yours truly, chatting away until I hear the snuffle of her sleep. But that has been the situation for some time, and I will do what is required to ensure that her door will remain open to me; I have not the will to break it down. For the most part, in my company, day and night, she is silent and I am thankful for that.

This is not to say that she is silent all the time. On occasion, she will break into laughter, trilling up and down the scale, and for no discernible reason. At these times she will twist her curls and dance wildly about the room. She will seize little Jane and swing her much too high. She will seize Elizabeth and fling her about the room singing a silly song about pretty little maidens and dashing young lads, her eyes wild with excitement. She pays inordinate attention to the girls' appearance, especially Jane's, always fussing with their dresses, their hair, their manners. She herself dresses differently in recent months: she wears the clothes of a young girl; she dresses her hair as if she were a girl—curls and ribbons abound. On the other hand, during her silent periods, she withdraws into drabness: she pays no heed to her appearance whatsoever; she dresses all in grey. Indeed, recently the girls have avoided her; they do not know what to make of their mother's change in moods. Nor do I. Nor does Mrs. Rummidge. Of all people in our household I would have thought that Mrs. Rummidge would have been able to take her in hand. But no, and so Mrs. Rummidge, after all these years, has thrown up her hands and removed herself from Longbourn, wailing loudly as she did about the ingratitude of her little lamb—

that would be Mrs. Bennet—and the loving attentions from her own wee bairns, who I doubt exist. Strange to say, but I will miss her. As do the children.

I have asked Mrs. Bennet's sister, Jane, to visit. I have known her to be in all ways a sensible woman. She is a great favourite of Mrs. Bennet's. My hope is that she can restore to my wife a certain steadiness of mind. I do not expect her to discover the cause of her current rocky state; such would not be advisable. But I will do what I can to help Jane return my wife to a lucid state.

In recent months, then, I have repaired more and more frequently to my library. During the first days of her return I was contented enough in my wife's presence; I was agreeable to her suggestion that we walk about the garden. She seemed to appreciate my attempts at polite gossip when I informed her that Northfield had been closed, that the Millars had left the country and were not expected to return, perhaps ever. "That being the case," I said a bit triumphantly, "I will not be troubled with his trampling my hedges and treeing my foxes. For a while I feared having to take him to circuit court. He would not have enjoyed the attentions of the village onlookers at such a hearing." It may have been then, now that I think of it, that Marianne first fell into a silence that was unsettling. I cannot be sure but it was not long after that episode that she ignored my invitations to walk about the property and began spending much of the day in her rooms, that is, when she was not twirling and whirling about in the drawing room. Since then I have never known what to expect from her except a distancing from me and from the children, no matter her exuberance or her withdrawal from life.

And so to my library. It holds not love or passion, but it does hold solace, and what more can a man wish for in this sorry world? *The Anatomy of Melancholy* will be my constant companion for want of any other.

Still, I remind myself in this my final entry that in this very year Mrs. Bennet will turn nineteen. Perhaps maturity will bring peace to us all.

13 March 1788

Ch. 42

Dear Jane,

Please hurry. You are my only hope for salvation. You are the only one who knows of the destruction I have brought upon myself, and yet even you cannot understand the depth of it, the damage of it. I am a husk. I have been scoured out. My flesh is stone and I cannot feel the touch even of my own children. I am no good to anyone nor they to me. At first, upon my return from that wicked city whose name shall never again pass my lips, I took a certain pleasure in assuming my roles as wife, mother, and mistress of the hearth. With the end of the harsh winter, I enjoyed long walks along the paths, dark, green, and cool, overarched with trees, snapdragons rising alongside, roses and hyacinths lovely and reminding me that life in the country has much to recommend it.

My good intentions—helping the poor and needy—have

gone by the wayside, for I have decided that I must avoid the village, for fear of unfriendly whispers. It is well known that servants' main source of pleasure is gossip about their superiors; it is less well known that gossip can travel long distances. I fear that some of Mrs. Littleworth's servants may have returned from Bath with their mistress; if so, news of my ill fortune will have traveled with them. Indeed, I have seen in my own household some of my servants—especially Hildy, the serving wench who seduced our cousin Collins—looking at me in such a way that makes my skin grow cold. Fortunately, that is all—just the looking—and no one has had the courage to charge me outright with whatever their suspicions might be.

However wise my intentions, the time came when duty bound me to go to the village. I had suspicions of my own, one being that the new kitchen maid, charged with securing foodstuffs in the village, was paying out more money than Cook had in her earlier visits to town. And so I followed Thelma—such an unfortunate name—into the village, where, sure enough, I witnessed her pocketing a goodly sum which I knew she would deny if confronted. And so she would have, but because I saw and heard her exchange with the tradesmen—they requested exactly the same as they had of Cook, leaving this wretched girl free to claim to me once we were back at Longbourn that prices had risen, that she had no leftover funds to return to me—I simply discharged her then and there in full view of the farmers and tradesmen. Off she went, shaking her fist at me and hurling curses into the air. I maintained my composure and ventured on with head held high. I do believe that my action rendered my reputation among the villagers, if sullied by gossip, respectable once more, or at least less odious. Back at Longbourn I did not bother to tell Mr. Bennet of the incident, even though my tale would speak to my ability to run his household in accordance with his wishes and thus open his eyes to my new maturity. His approval, so long withheld, no longer mattered to me.

Something of import did, however, transpire during that visit. As I followed Thelma, darting behind barrels and wagons so as not to be noticed, I saw the loathsome Mrs. Littleworth coming toward me. How could I have thought her sophisticated, well dressed, even chic? Apparently she had taken up her husband's pastime—eating—for she was at least two stone heavier than when last I saw her; indeed, she lumbered as she approached. The closer she came the more I could see that the seams in her gown were close to bursting. Still, there remained about her an aura of the class to which she had been born. No matter that her husband was an idiot, no matter that her dress was an embarrassment, her head was held higher than mine could ever go, so high that she seemed scarcely to see me. She gazed at something over my head, and I prayed that she would pass by without noticing me. If she didn't, if she paused, if she looked down to where I was, what in heaven's name was I to do? What to say?

My prayers went unanswered. She advanced on me until, had she not paused, she would have run me over. But pause she did and from her great height she addressed not me but her husband. "Ah yes, it is little Mrs. Bennet, mistress of Longbourn, I believe. Say good day, Mr. Littleworth." He did and reminded Mrs. Littleworth that they were late for tea. She remained rooted to the spot, as if she was sorting out a condemnation to throw at my head, and so Mr. Littleworth was forced to speak again. This time, without his wife's prodding, he spoke directly to me. "My wife and I have settled for the last time. No travel, none; we are at home only to our friends, most of whom have departed this earth for the last time. We—Mrs. L. and I—are content to await our final last time at home." Mrs. Littleworth looked anything but contented and I felt enormous pleasure at the thought that she would spend the rest of her life a prisoner in her own grand abode with her ridiculous husband her jailer. And yet they tarried so that I was forced to speak. What came to me was, What news have you of the colonel? What I said was, "Good day to you both. I will give Mr. Bennet your good wishes." With this, they resumed their walk, and I returned to Longbourn. And that's where I stayed, choosing to take my walk on paths nearby, paths that no one would traipse but me, paths where I was safe from discovery and the opprobrium that would surely follow. Mrs. Littleworth would never find me there.

Soon, though, I left off my walking; I found it no longer pleased me. One day in a fit of ill humour, I plucked the stone from my shoe and hurled it into the wood. And I became nothing.

Duty. That is what is left to me. To do my duty I must destroy the memory of him, bury it deep within; for when I do not, when I cannot, the memory of his touch, his voice, his smile brings to me once more the full surge of passion that comes from deep inside me and floods my whole being. I must not allow memory to surface. I must deny it. I must deny myself. And you must help. I beg of you, else I shall go mad.

In moments of clarity, I believe that, with your help, the life ahead of me promises great rewards should I prove myself worthy of them. How I yearn to be thought worthy in someone's eyes, anyone's eyes. It seems that I am out of favour with everyone and I am exceedingly lonely. Who is at fault, you might ask. Mr. Bennet? Mrs. Littleworth? My colonel? No, it is I. I am to blame for the empty life that is mine and for the unhappiness of my husband and children, though if fate is kind, my little girls are not yet so sorely tainted. To remedy this dreadful situation, I intend to work to ensure that this home becomes free of entailment, that it belongs to my husband in perpetuity; and I shall do this by bringing up my daughters to be splendid wives of stalwart young men in possession of good fortune. Then we shall all live happily ever after.

Yr sister,

Marianne

Ch. 43

Yet another entry, this one with no wise prologue.

Jane's visit, while providing me excellent company and the children the kindly attention they hungered for, did nothing to alleviate Mrs. Bennet's illness. Here is a woman, I often thought of Jane, of substance, a kind companion, calm in the storms of temper exhibited by her sister, soothing to her and to me. Here is a woman who might have made me a most suitable wife. Alas, too late, and I have had to remind myself to leave off such longings. As for my wife, I am at a loss to explain her behaviour as anything other than that, an illness for which apparently there is no cure. To my regret, Jane returned to her home much the sadder, for she, too, was forced to admit that her efforts to restore her sister to reason were for naught.

I retreat further into my study and contemplate carving into my bookshelves those words which Montaigne, on his thirty-eighth birthday, carved into his own shelves when he retired forever into his library: "Michel de Montaigne . . . will [here] spend what little remains of his life, now more than half run out. If the fates permit, he will complete this abode, this sweet ancestral retreat; and he has consecrated it to his freedom, tranquillity, and leisure." As will I.

Ch. 44

Dear Jane,

I write this hastily, while I am in my right mind; I cannot predict how long that might be. But I wish you to know that I do not blame you for abandoning me to my empty life at Longbourn. Try though I might, I could not succeed in restoring my virtue; instead, my conduct was such that it did not recommend itself to those unfortunate enough to be in its path. You, I fear, were its foremost victim, my husband and children having accustomed themselves more or less to the aberrations that I presented. Indeed, since your departure, they see to it that they live their lives as separate from me as possible. For me it is too late; I pray that it is not so for them.

My children, whose affection I have always enjoyed, avoid me; thus, I am quite alone although never so alone as when I place myself in their midst and demand that we all dance or sing or skip about. One would think that children would take readily to my suggestion, but my children do not; instead, they shy away from me. Only yesterday, thinking to remedy this sad situation, I picked up my Jane and began to dance, to waltz. One-two-three, one-two-three, I dipped and turned until even my head was spinning. Elizabeth from the sideline began to cry, out of envy, I suppose; Jane screeched in delight, but just as we were waltzing our way into the foyer, Mr. Bennet burst forth from his library and with that strong arm of his swept Jane from my arms. "See how silly your mother is today," he said. Elizabeth pointed at me and repeated, "Mama silly."

Increasingly, I choose not to help myself, for while I have only to listen to those around me to know that I am behaving foolishly and ought to shake myself free of such nonsensical behaviour, I prefer flightiness to despair; if I can maintain the former during the day, I can almost endure the nighttime, when the emptiness of my soul drives me further into the latter. Surely I am doing a good turn by my silliness; better that than the grave demeanour which is its opposite. At least, I am providing my children with a semblance of feminine behaviour, a model to emulate as they grow into womanhood. Or perhaps not, I do not know.

The truth is, dear Jane, that I do not know who I ought to be or who I am any more than I did in the years when we were but girls. In these dark hours, in the absence of soul and spirit, I am incapable of denying memory its presence. It is a constant shadow which, come evening, spreads itself over all and sends me to my bedchamber, where it falls upon me like a cloak too heavy to throw off. And, like a spirit unbound, in he comes to torture me with memories of his touch, of his voice, of his very body as we lie together. Memory is my true punishment; would that I knew when or if it would end.

I would confess to the world at large that I did wrong if I believed that doing so would send memory scurrying away. I would confess that my unthinking behaviour threatened my marriage, that I humiliated my husband, and that I risked even the love of my children. And I have tried. I have wept alone. I have begged there in the darkness to be forgiven. I have promised myself to change my ways, to re-make myself in the image of you, Jane, to cast out the demon in me that has led to so much grief. My efforts have been to no avail. Morning finds me exhausted and without hope of restoration.

I am incapable of my own life.

And so I shall adopt another. You, in your most sisterly fashion, believing that speaking forthrightly to me would accomplish what your letters have not, proceeded to upbraid me for being foolish. Mr. Bennet, too, thinks I am but a silly woman. My children agree. Likewise Mrs. Littleworth. And most painfully, Colonel Millar. Well, if that is what you think of me, then that is what I shall be: forever a girl, never a woman. Silly. Foolish. Unworthy of serious concern.

Let us see what comes of that.

Marianne Bennet

Afterword

How in the world did this novel come to be? I am still amazed that it exists and that I wrote it. I was never an ardent fan of Jane Austen's novels, though I had read them with pleasure. Still, I had no particular interest in reviving Mrs. Bennet and was quite content with the 1940 film starring Greer Garson and Laurence Olivier. I adored it, in fact, and nobody since, except for Colin Firth, comes close to Sir Laurence's Darcy. Granted, Greer Garson is not the perfect Elizabeth, but Keira Knightley? Too skinny. Jennifer Ehle? Coarse. And the other Darcys? I don't even remember their names.

Let's blame this novel on feminism. It got hold of me sometime in the 1970s and has never let go. I was not a bra burner, nor did I join my sisters on the kitchen table where with mirrors aplenty they viewed their private parts. I did not march for women's rights, though I don't remember anyone asking me. I didn't make speeches, though if they had asked me, I wouldn't have known what to say. Yet things were not the same; I began to think about the girls and women in literature and in magazines of the day and I began to say, Wait a minute, let's take another look at Curley's wife in *Of Mice and Men*. Let's take another look at Hester Prynne and at Anna Karenina and at Scout Finch. Doing that made life—and teaching—infinitely more interesting.

So one day, around 2009, primed by forty years of feminist wondering, I was taking a walk and thinking. With me was William, the man to whom this novel is dedicated. Always when we walk we wonder about a lot of things: how to write a bestseller, whether or not Kafka is overrated, how many people have actually read *Moby Dick*, and who is the sexiest writer in South America. On this particular day, I said, "You know, I think Mrs. Bennet got a bad deal." And because I had been thinking about this for some time, I said, "Five children in eight years is enough to unsettle anybody. On the other hand, maybe she was always dotty, or do you think she got that way after she married Mr. Bennet or only as all those daughters were being born?" And William said, "There's your novel."

And so it was. Of course, I nay-said the whole ridiculous thing: I didn't know how to write a novel, it would take too long even if I tried, and I knew nothing about the particulars of that century. Best to drop the whole thing. However, I needed to find the answer to my question! So I reread *Pride and Prejudice*, this time searching for clues. Why, Jane Austen hadn't even given Mrs. Bennet a first name, let alone told us how old she was when she married!

Then, on another walk, alone this time, the first line came to me: "O la! If only poor Mother had lived to tell me of the infamy that would be my wedding night." The rest is what you have read, and I thank you for doing so. I hope you were pleased. Or amused. Not bored. Not upset. I hope you are smiling.

The lesson herein is: When puzzled, troubled, out of sorts, bored, angry, or happy as can be, take a walk. Something will happen.